STAR-PACKER'S LUCK

A body is dumped outside the law office of Canyon Pass, and Sheriff Ep Lamister investigates. Then Pete Torlando and his boys pull off a bloody robbery, a young outlaw is mauled by a wild cat and apprehended, and a wild lady and her paramour join the gang in a jail break. Now a wounded star-packer is on the vengeance trail. Killing follows bloody killing, until a gang leader and a sheriff face each other for the final, deadly showdown . . .

Books by Vic J. Hanson
in the Linford Western Library:

KILLER ALONE
SILVO
KILLER'S HARVEST
HARDISTY'S TOWN
A LONER'S REVENGE
BLACKSNAKE TRAIL

VIC J. HANSON

STAR-PACKER'S LUCK

Complete and Unabridged

LINFORD
Leicester

First published in Great Britain in 1999 by
Robert Hale Limited
London

First Linford Edition
published 2002
by arrangement with
Robert Hale Limited
London

British Library CIP Data

Hanson, Vic J.
    Star-packer's luck.—Large print ed.—
Linford western library
1. Western stories
2. Large type books
I. Title
823.9'14 [F]

ISBN 0–7089–9868–2

Published by
F. A. Thorpe (Publishing)
Anstey, Leicestershire

Set by Words & Graphics Ltd.
Anstey, Leicestershire
Printed and bound in Great Britain by
T. J. International Ltd., Padstow, Cornwall

1

Sheriff Lamister heard the thump outside the office door but didn't take much notice of it. A falling down drunk!

He had heard folks go by and the sound of hooves. There was still noise from the saloon down the street, but the night was slowly becoming quiet.

He was taking things easy, would be going out on night duty as soon as his deputy, Denny, returned after an evening with his cronies. Taking a pattern from his chief, Denny knew all sorts of folk, as a Western lawman should.

Though still a mite restless, the deputy was turning out to be pretty good at his job.

Boot-heels clattered outside, and then the tall, lean young man came through the door and said, 'There's a body outside on the stoop.'

Ep Lamister rose to his feet, could already hear more noise from outside as if folks were gathering.

'Shot in the head,' said Denny. 'Close range. He ain't very recognizable. The light ain't too good out there anyway.'

Ep said, 'I didn't hear a shot.'

'Me neither. I guess nobody did. Blood's drying. None around the body.'

'Get the lantern an' bring it out here.' Ep moved to the door, opened it wide.

There were a cluster of folk. They parted to let him by and he asked, 'Anybody recognize him?'

Seemed like nobody did — not yet anyway.

Denny brought the lantern out. Its rays illuminated the street, the stoop, the staring, yammering faces, the crumpled body.

'Looks kinda familiar,' said somebody, but added no more. Somebody else commented, 'Face is kinda spoiled.'

And that was sort of an understatement.

They took the body down to the undertaker's parlour, waking up its lugubrious custodian. During the day, poised over his inarticulate customers, he could be quite jolly. But he was a drinking man, had imbibed much this night. Eyes bleary, he yowled, 'Gimme room.'

There was plenty of light now. Somebody had lit the hanging lantern over the trestle on which the body had been placed, partly straightened but still not an enlightening sight. But Ep Lamister, bending closer, said, 'I know him.'

'So do I,' said undertaker Dickie Moley, brightening. 'That's Jo-Jo MacTeen.'

'You're right, bucko. See that patch o' bald skin over his left ear, and the scar there? Jo-Jo got creased by a rifle bullet when me an' him were after the Drifter brothers.'

'You got 'em, though,' said Deputy Denny Trape.

'That was before Jo-Jo turned bad,' said the undertaker. 'I'll clean him up.'

Sheriff Lamister said, 'We'll get the doc. Maybe he'll be able to figure how long Jo-Jo's been dead.'

'A while I guess,' said Dickie Moley. 'Gimme room, all o' yuh.'

He was youngish, tallish, burly. When the doc appeared he greeted him like an old friend, which he was, a sort of uncle to many of the younger folks hereabouts. He was small and fox-grey and was called Doc Jock, him being a Scot an' all, still with that friendly burr to his voice.

* * *

Ep and Denny rode in the early morning. The sheriff said, 'It's gonna be another hot one like it was yesterday.'

'That certainly messed-up Doc Jock's figuring on the body,' Denny said, added. 'But murder is usually a night thing, ain't it?'

'Not always. And that one looked like

4

it was a sort of execution.'

The gates of the Cross Kettle Ranch were plain to their sight. Then they could see the two men, each with a rifle, standing, well-separated in the wide space between the heavy, thrown-back crossbars.

Denny said, 'I didn't know ol' Bogal had guards out here.'

'He don't usually.' Ep raised his hand over his head in the time-honoured peace signal.

The two riflemen leaned forward, peering, one of them shading his eyes against the glare of the burgeoning sun. He turned his head and spoke to his companion and they both lowered their weapons. The two horsemen reached them. They exchanged greetings, then one of the rannies said, 'Had rustlers last night sheriff. Got away with quite a slew of beef. The boss was comin' out to see you.'

'Here he comes,' said the other ranny and the surrey with the two ponies came bowling down the drive.

Rancher Bogal was alone, bull-shouldered, long white hair escaping from beneath his smart pearl-grey Stetson.

'You heard, Ep?'

'Only just,' said the sheriff. 'Was comin' on another matter.'

'Best go back to the house then.' Simon Bogal wheeled the equipage around, the two prime ponies stepping lively. 'You two boys stay here till you're relieved.'

The guards moved apart, turned back towards the trail, rifles at ready again.

The Cross Kettle was the biggest ranch by far in this territory. There were folks who complained that Simon Bogal would like to take over the neighbouring town of Canyon Pass as part of his holdings, running cattle everyplace, and down along the narrow creek and the low-lying pass that had given the place its name.

Some of the Kettle boys acted like they already owned the town. Sheriff

Lamister aimed to keep the peace there and, so far, hadn't done badly. Simon Bogal was an old friend, but no favours were owed to *him*.

Ep waited to hear Simon's story before telling his own, and asking questions. Murder. Mayhem. Rustling ... Maybe the whole caboodle was connected by threads. Either weak or strong.

Or maybe not at all ...

2

Stefan took the gold half-hunter carefully from his vest pocket. As far as he knew, this was the first time the chief had lent it out to anybody.

The chief had taken the watch with the heavy gold chain from a passenger in a stagecoach hold-up. Stefan hadn't been there at the time, had been younger, hadn't even known the chief.

As Stefan had heard, during that robbery nobody had been hurt unnecessarily, shot that is.

There had been a nasty killing yesterday, though.

Stefan tried not to think about that.

The chief, Pete Torlando, was wanted by the law along the borderlands. Stefan, an orphan who'd been dragged around by his boot-heels, was mighty proud to be one of Torlando's boys. He was the youngest in the six-man gang.

Counting the chief. But no, even that wasn't right — not now. There had been six till the killing yesterday. Now there were just five, counting Stefan himself.

Pete Torlando had earlier found a grassy draw on the edge of the badlands. The stolen cattle grazed there now, out of sight, in Stefan's charge. Torlando had told Stefan that if he saw strange riders approaching he should get out of there, leave the beef. Also, if Torlando and the rest of the boys didn't return at the given time he, Stefan, was to get out of there anyway and go to the arranged rendezvous. 'Leave the beef,' Torlando had said, chuckling, 'that'll puzzle some folk all to hell an' back.'

Stefan wasn't good at telling the time, half-hunter or no half-hunter, but he figured it was time the boys got back.

At the back of the draw, facing out to the badlands, not the grasslands on the other side, there was a small pool and the cattle were browsing there. It had been drying up in the recent blazing sun but there was still some muddy water in its bottoms. Stefan figured that he couldn't be spotted from the good end of the draw, unless those stupid critters started to bawl. The chief had sure picked this place well.

Stefan didn't know what the chief and the boys were doing now, but he reckoned that it had something to do with a town called Canyon Pass. He was an untutored cuss, and he knew it — but his mind was always active. Sometimes he wished to hell it wasn't.

He could not stop *thinking*.

His mind kept going back to the time of the killing, the way the killing had been done, making his blood run cold. He had never shot at a human being, let alone killed one. But the man who had done the killing was a man who enjoyed killing, had seen the chance, taken it.

★　★　★

The stagecoach was the largest and grandest that the boys had ever seen.

Nobody could have imagined that it would carry anything but the smartest and most well-britched of passengers, and with no common freight at all.

The coach that the boys looked out upon from their concealed positions had three men up top on a seat which was wider than usual. One held the reins. Although the other two were bolt upright they didn't have any weapons in plain sight. Baggage-handlers? Nah, Pete Torlando and his boys didn't think so.

Coming along the narrow trail, the carriage looked like part of a puffing billy, but with no puffer.

A train could have been used, of course, but the dispatchers of this particular vehicle had been cleverer than that. Trains could be held up and lots of passengers put in jeopardy. The dispatchers had, in fact, been mighty cunning. Stagecoaches didn't usually run on this particular trail, and not much else either. The track was narrow, undulating and very rough.

The equipage came on slowly and the four men waited, their horses browsing, hidden, not far behind them.

The palatial coach, approaching, was obviously strongly built and well-sprung, probably specially built for its purpose. Were some of its passengers, glimpsed now by the hidden, waiting road agents, sort of special, too?

But it was too late to worry about that now.

'Take 'em,' said Pete Torlando.

★ ★ ★

Beef had vanished as if the grasslands had swallowed them. Nobody had seen or heard anything. Sheriff Lamister had said to Denny Trape as they returned to town, 'Let that bullheaded ol' cuss, Simon Bogal, look after his own bailiwick.' There were no more items of news awaiting the two lawmen in Canyon Pass. Their main task, finding the killer of Jo-Jo MacTeen, was no further forward.

Back at Cross Kettle Ranch nobody had seen strangers in the territory, neither rustlers or killers, whether one and the same or not.

While Ep and Denny were absent, the jailhouse, though it was empty, had been looked after by the 'second deputy', Tubs Smildey, who said, 'So you got nothing?'

'You get outa here, bucko,' said his chief. 'Go take a *pasear*. You might even pick up somep'n.'

'Fat chance,' Tubs retorted.

He was a short man with a round belly, a jowly, jolly face and a shock of white hair. Brought up in this territory, he'd been called Tubs since his schooldays and didn't mind a bit. He was somewhat older than Ep Lamister, but they'd been kids together. Tubs had married a local girl called Dulcie. Later, Ep had married Dulcie's sister, Edna.

Edna had died after bearing her first child, a son. The baby had died also. Ep hadn't remarried, lived alone adjacent to the jail.

Dulcie and Tubs still shared their frame house on the edge of town. Their only son ran the local gunshop in which his father had a share in order to supplement his deputy's mediocre pay.

Tubs Smildey didn't go for a walkabout that day, a *pasear* as his old friend Ep had suggested. He got his horse and went for a ride. He loved riding.

Ep and Denny had only been to the big ranch, not to the smallholdings that were dotted around the edge of the Cross Kettle's wide-stretched range-lands. Tubs did the rounds, drank a lot of coffee, ate pecan pie at one place, hotcakes at another, smoked from various makings, including Mexican weed from a farmer called Curly Joe.

His rawboned mare, Kitty, had some good water and fair to middlin' hay and made a few stallions go skittish. But, all in all, Tubs didn't learn a lot and turned back for home.

3

The two men on a box seat of the stagecoach, with the hackey in between them, both drew guns, one a long-barrelled hand weapon that looked like a Dragoon Colt, the other a double-snouted 12 gauge that he must have had hidden down by his feet.

The man in between, who hadn't been pushing the four horses to any sort of big speed, dropped the reins and brought out a pistol which wasn't as big as either of his companions' weapons but undeniably just as lethal.

Three men had come out of the rocks on one side. One man had come out as back-up — a surprise third — from the other side of the rocky narrow trail. This was Torlando's murderous *segundo*, Brazos Tom, who yelled, 'Drop 'em, boys.'

Two of the men on the box seat

swivelled their heads from one direction to the other. Neither of the other three hold-up men had said a word. But, like somebody had once said, Brazos Tom had always been a mouthy bastard.

The stage driver leaned forward from between his two partners and raised his pistol. Tom shot him in the throat, banging him against the guard with the shotgun, who also had his gaze turned in Tom's direction.

Whether by accident or design, the shotgun exploded with both barrels at once. The charge took Brazos Tom's shoulder off in a mess of blood and bone, knocking him back in the rocks like he had been kicked by all four of the now restive horses.

One of his guns went off, the slug whining into the air.

Hidden from sight, Tom had passed out.

As the echoes died, Pete Torlando shouted, 'Hold it, all o' yuh.'

The shotgun guard had been spattered with the driver's blood. He had pushed the body away from him and it now leaned forward as if the man was still alive and was taking a great interest in his horses' rumps, which were almost still now. And the wheels had stopped turning. The third man dropped his long-barrelled Colt. Both men raised their hands in the air.

Torlando kept the two men covered while his two boys moved up to the side of the coach, where shocked faces peered, and ordered the passengers to climb down.

Torlando gestured with his guns. The two unarmed men got down. The dead driver remained in his seat. A glance past the horses' snouts had made the bandit leader surmise that his pard Brazos Tom wasn't about to rise up from the rocks.

Small wooden steps were let down from the coach. The passengers alighted one by one. Torlando called one of his men back, told him to climb up on to the box seat. The man did this, shoving the dead body violently aside and out of sight, to share a rock-strewn space with the one who had shot him.

The man found a padlock at the back of the box seat. His gun blasted. Fragments of steel flew, with pieces of blanket cushion.

The man lifted the lid and gave an obscenely delighted exclamation.

The third man had the passengers lined up.

But he wasn't vigilant enough.

Things happened with explosive rapidity . . .

A young woman sobbing. An older one trying to comfort her. Two elderly men who looked like Eastern business types. A weedy youth who looked plain scared.

The bandits wanted valuables. All they could get. Most folks, menaced, shocked, were mighty co-operative.

Two females. Three males at first. Then the last one. Didn't look much. Slow, awkward, gangling, about thirty.

The stick-up man, a two-gun toter, who had holstered one of his weapons and had a burlap sack in his free hand, was jabbering hotly at the two elderly gents. Chief Torlando and his partner, up at the other end of the coach with the two guards and the four horses, couldn't hear what was being said.

One of the elderly business types was answering back. The aggressor with the burlap sack raised his gun threateningly with his other hand. This was when the gangling feller who'd just got down from the carriage went off like a firecracker.

Guns had been gathered, or so it seemed. But the gangling feller had a Bulldog pistol in a shoulder holster under his dark broadcloth coat, and he pulled that weapon like it was slick with pig grease, fired it. The hold-up man was hit in the chest at close range and went flat on his back like he'd been pushed by an invisible battering ram.

The fast man, not gangling any more, whirled towards the other end of the coach. But he'd lost his edge. The bandit leader had a shooter pointing straight at him and was thumbing the hammer.

A bullet in his temple, the courageous gunfighting passenger collapsed atop the bandit he had himself brought down.

Two corpses in a last embrace. And Pete Torlando yelling at his companion: 'Watch 'em. I'll get that box down.'

The other man descended from his perch. He'd have no more trouble with the other passengers. Nobody was arguing with anybody any more. The young woman had fainted and the older one was bending over her. The two elderly gents and the weedy youth were as still as if suddenly turned to stone.

Torlando managed to lift the heavy box and slide it down to the ground. He called, 'Shepherd 'em inside and shut the door. Bring that sack. Tell 'em if they show their heads outside the coach we'll pepper 'em.'

The passengers heard this, and there was a scramble. Everybody tried to get the unconscious young woman on first, finally managing this. The road agent shut the door.

Then, gun in one hand, burlap sack in the other, that man joined the chief who said, 'Go check on Brazos Tom.'

The man crossed the trail under the noses of the four horses, the two guards held at bay. He bent over the rocks, shook his head from side to side, turned and retraced his steps.

'Fetch the horses.'

Again the other man did as was ordered. He was smaller than Torlando and a mite older. He was called Soddie Bill. It was said he'd been born in the ground. He had really been weaned in a soddie against a hill, his mother a whore, his father a roamer who came back to his sorry billet from time to time.

'Merry days,' Bill said now. It was a favourite saying of his. He had a peculiar sense of humour.

4

Deputy Tubs Smildey heard the crackle of gunfire in the distance, carried to him on the breeze. He had been on his way back to Canyon Pass but now he turned his horse to the right, a wary man, taking it easy.

He approached the rocks which screened the old trail, the one that nobody ever used nowadays. There was no noise now except the soughing of the breeze but Tubs, exposed as he was, didn't aim to take chances. He drew his long-barrelled Remington pistol and held it across the front of his saddle.

He was almost upon the jumbled, craggy rocks when a figure rose up from among them. In a vague sort of way. Like a spirit that had found itself in an unknown and lonely place.

But this apparition came in the shape of a seedy-looking young man in garments that Tubs immediately thought of as Eastern, the only Western thing about the spectre being the chunky Bulldog pistol held in a thin fist.

Tubs raised his own gun, said quietly, 'Easy now, drop that, son, if you please.'

The young man dropped it, said, 'It wasn't mine,' adding, 'There are two men tied up here,' making a backward gesture with a limp hand. 'And — and people are dead. Bandits — they got away.'

Tubs dismounted, went quickly past the younker. The two men lay side by side in the brittle grass, both trussed with rawhide, though one of them had gotten his legs free.

'Help me,' said Tubs, over his shoulder. 'Quickly.'

It was done. The two men rose, chafing their sore wrists, murmuring thanks. Tubs didn't know either of them. He followed their stiff progress to the scene of the killings alongside the grotesque stagecoach he hadn't seen the like of before.

A dead shotgun guard who had been dragged to the others. The fallen road agent. The body of the young man who'd shot him. One of the two elderly business-looking gents who were still alive saying, 'He was too brave. Too pitifully brave.' A sentiment that was echoed by two women, young and old, the latter with her arms round her companion who looked as if she'd recently come out of a faint.

Back at the head of the coach where the horses stood with heads hanging, one of the Westerners shouted, 'There's another of them scumbags back hyar.'

Tubs went back to them where they were in the rocks bending over a man with his shoulder literally blown away, blood all over him.

Tubs took out his deputy's star and pinned it on his breast. He usually didn't reveal it during his off-duty times. But he had walked into a bloody mess of trouble and carnage here all right!

He got down on one knee, grabbed a limp wrist. 'This'n's still alive,' he pronounced. Then he asked, 'What were they after?'

'A long strongbox.'

'What was in it?'

'We don't know.'

Then, from behind, another spoke up, indignantly. 'We were not told we were travelling in a treasure wagon.' It was one of the elderly business-type gents, going on, 'The company said this would be the first trip on this brand new coach of theirs, said they wanted it tested over this old trail. We paid over the damned odds for this maiden voyage . . . ' The sarcastic voice died away.

Tubs said, jerking a thumb, 'Maybe this'n will be able to talk.'

One of the coachmen said, 'I doubt it, Deppity. But I've got some bandages an' stuff, allus carry some.' He turned away.

Tubs said, 'We'll go to Canyon Pass.'

The second coachman said, 'We were

supposed to bypass that town.'

His partner returned with a wicker basket which he held forth to reveal the medical objects he'd spoken about. 'We have three bodies. We can put 'em in the big luggage place back o' the coach. There'll be room there.'

They all turned as they heard a clattering and thumping from the rocks behind. Tubs drew his gun, lowered it. The weedy youth appeared dragging a long wooden box.

'It's empty,' he said. Behind him appeared a friendly-looking riderless horse.

'Put it down, son,' said Deputy Tubs and holstered his gun again.

It was decided that the three bodies would go in back of the long coach. The wounded man, after being patched up, would go on the spare horse. The empty box would go up behind the four horses where it had been before, the two coachmen sitting on it.

After the body of the brave young man who had braced and killed one of the bandits had been laid in its place there was no more lament from the girl who had recovered from her vapours, though she was still under the watchful eyes of her companion.

Tubs Smildey took the place on the box which had earlier been occupied by the late hackey with the shotgun. The blood had dried. One of the coachmen, from his perch, held the reins and guided the spare horse, now occupied with the bandage and roped-on wounded bandit.

* * *

The wildcat came upon the rocks, heard the cattle on the other side, smelled them, licked her parched lips. Her nostrils flared: she sensed water too. She slunk through the rocks on her belly. The stupid longhorns were restless.

She saw them, became immediately still, lay with her paws flat and her chin upon them, her belly and legs stretched, feeling the heat of the hot rocks, the glare of the sun on her muscled back.

She saw the man. He was turned away from her. He had one of those long, shining things that made a noise, though this one was noiseless now. Such a thing had killed her mate, and she and her babies had taken to the badlands. But pickings were meagre there.

She couldn't now hear the whimperings of her cubs. Her own hunger and thirst was the driving force, and it grew as she saw two dogies in the herd.

Still on her belly, she moved on the longhorns and they became even more restive. She circled them slowly, smoothly, cunningly, and they began to move, spread, but did not start to scatter. She could not get at the dogies.

The bulk of the cattle was between her and the small pool.

Some sense warned the young man, who called himself Stefan, and he turned, raising the rifle.

His movement caused the wildcat to

whirl, raising herself, and then to leap desperately at him, remembering what had happened to her mate.

She hit the young man low, her claws unsheathed, raking him across the hips and crotch. Falling backwards, he screamed. His finger contracted on the trigger of the Winchester and it went off, awakening the echoes.

★ ★ ★

Rancher Simon Bogal and his boys had gotten themselves an Indian tracker dubbed Silencio. The sudden shot in the hot, still air brought him to a halt, his boss right behind him. They saw the startled beef milling out of the rocks, the two dogies trying to keep up with the rest.

The cattle, confronted suddenly by men on horseback, didn't know which way to turn; and they turned in on themselves, serving as cover for the approaching ranchmen.

The boys soon found the youngster,

his rifle away from him. He was too torn-up to do anything with it anyway, but he and his weapon had paid their dues: the dead wildcat, shot in the front of the head, lay at the young man's feet.

The clawed younker had passed out. Gazing down at him, one of the rannies said, 'No cathouse frail's gonna look on him kindly for a while — if ever.'

'Quit your damn' lollygaggin',' said the boss. 'Get that beef together.'

The cowboys hastened to do his bidding. Silencio grabbed the dead wildcat, dragged it into the rocks and dumped it. Then, with the stuff he had gotten from his own warbag and those of his friends, the elderly Yaqui Indian did what he could with the unconscious and badly hurt younker.

The boss would want this cuss to talk. But Silencio was mighty dubious about that.

5

Pete Torlando said, 'I told young Stefan to show himself and wave as soon as he saw us.'

Soddie Bill said, 'Maybe he took off.'

Torlando said, 'Wait . . . ' They saw the cattle coming out of the rocks, and two men, maybe more.

'We'll split up, go round back. Move!'

Torlando put spurs to his horse, and Bill followed suit. The other men were unmounted and chivvying the cattle, so the two outlaws had the edge on them. But one of the cowboys, quick, head turning, raised his rifle. Then he couldn't see anything to shoot at. The two strange horsemen were hidden by the rocks as they skirted them, making for the badlands like the hordes of Hades were at their heels.

They had plenty of water and tucker. Torlando had made sure of that, figuring they'd mostly have to use the wild sparse lands for a getaway with their loot, and maybe the cattle as well. But no hardship yet! There would be pursuers. But, certainly, those cowmen wouldn't have come prepared.

In truth, the outlaw leader's figuring was ace-high. A bunch under the leadership of Simon Bogal followed the fugitives while some others took the beef back to the ranch. But then, their quarry out of their sight, the ranch boss halted his mount, stopping his followers, and said, 'We ain't fixed for this, didn't expect it. We'll have to try again, make time.'

They knew him, knew he meant what he said. Robbers should be eliminated, so that they could never come back.

* * *

Soddie Bill reached for his canteen, lifted it, took a big swig.

Torlando said, 'Go easy on that. I'm

telling yuh! We've got a hell of a long way to go yet.'

Bill stoppered the canteen, let it dangle. Damn' boss-man! But Torlando was always right. Or was he?

Bill couldn't help wondering about young Stefan. He had always thought that that younker was too mealy-mouthed. If he'd been captured maybe he'd talk.

Bill began to wonder about Brazos Tom also, the one he'd checked on, lying back in the rocks at the hold-up site with one shoulder reduced to bloody rags. Bill had told Torlando that Tom was finished — but he hadn't been sure himself. Tom was a tough little bastard. Would he be able to talk and, if he was, would he do just that?

Bill wasn't used to this much cogitating. His head began to ache. The sun didn't help either.

But what if anybody talked? What the hell! Him and the chief were on their way free — and mighty rich.

He didn't know their destination. But

he could be sure that Torlando had one. There was a lot Bill didn't know, figured he didn't know half as much as Brazos Tom had known, for Tom was — or had been — Torlando's *segundo*. That bloodthirsty bloodsoaked little heathen had been with Torlando a lot longer than Bill himself had.

Anyway, Bill had never wanted any part of any planning. Although he actually hated walking, he was a 'foot soldier', always had been. He did what Torlando said. He had oftimes done what Brazos Tom said, though he hated the man. Yeh, right now he hoped that Tom had finally handed in his pail.

The bareness around Soddie Bill and Pete Torlando was as if a plague had hit the land, scourging it, making it look like something that shouldn't be on earth, or on any other planet.

The sun had been above their heads, beating through their hats into their brains. Bill didn't know whether it had yet reached its zenith. It was a little in front of them now, its rays burning into his forehead.

He pulled his hat down. But then he couldn't see where he was going. He pushed the hat-brim back and the devilish hot rays branded his temples. He shaded his eyes with one hand, but then he could only see ahead of him into a sort of haze like pale smoke. He felt he was riding into this, and more, would suddenly be afire.

He reached for his canteen again, but then stopped himself. 'How far?' he croaked. 'How far?'

Torlando said, 'I guess we're about halfway.'

Remembering how hellishly far they had already travelled, Bill's heart sank. The sun was beating in his brain. He let his head sink on his chest and he could feel his heart beating, hear it like strangely ominous drumbeats.

Finally, he must have slept.

There was great heat — and then there was darkness and he thought he was dead.

Then he realized it was night.

Something was nudging him. Instinctively, he reached for his gun.

Torlando's harsh voice said, 'Wake up, idiot. Come alive, or you're gonna fall off your horse.'

As Bill straightened up, his chief's voice went on, 'We'll rest, take some sustenance. If anybody's got this far we'll hear 'em coming, but I don't figure for a moment that anybody has.'

They found a shallow dip into which the moon shone in a ghostly way.

Suddenly, Soddie Bill asked a question. Hell, why not? Wasn't Torlando his partner now?

'Why did Brazos Tom kill Jo-Jo MacTeen?'

'He had reasons, bucko. And I might say that Jo-Jo had already served his purpose.'

Bill gave a little spurt of dry and humourless laughter. 'Me an' Tom certainly dumped him in a place which would serve some kinda purpose, chief, I grant you that. Right in the law's lap in that town.' He hadn't particularly wanted to work with Brazos Tom, but it had been easy, they'd both figured that nobody spotted them.

'Y'know, chief, I sorta figured you might've known that sheriff of Canyon Pass.'

'Yeh. In the old days. And I've never sold 'im short. He's a prime lawman. And, y'know, Jo-Jo MacTeen was once one of his deppities.'

'Do tell!' exclaimed Bill in astonishment. 'No wonder Brazos Tom wanted to blow Jo-Jo's haid plumb off. An' he almost did, didn't he?'

Soon they were riding again under the pale moon, in the lesser heat, Torlando saying they'd make better time now and Bill feeling much better than he had been but, still an' all, wondering *what, where . . . ?*

Anyway, back there they'd given the law something to puzzle about and, in a different way, the ranch-folk also.

6

Undertaker Dickie Moley and old Doc Jock were back in business in Canyon Pass far more than they had expected to be so soon. Dickie's clients were very passive. It was the doc who had the harder tasks. The young rustler had been horribly clawed by the wildcat and had lost an enormous amount of blood. The same could be said for the grotesquely shotgun-wounded outlaw whom Sheriff Ep Lamister had identified as a Wanted killer known as Brazos Tom, a 'nasty little bastard tough as boots'. Tom had a fight on his hands; but the doc had figured he could do better for that one than he could for the younger category, more was the pity.

'Do your best, old friend,' the sheriff said. 'I certainly want one or the other of 'em to talk.'

Both patients were in a sort of

coma, but the heavyweight and cynical lawman said Brazos Tom might be playing possum. Irascible, Doc Jock said, 'I've got to keep him out an' work on that shoulder. Get out of here an' let me do my business. You do yours.'

Lamister went back to the witnesses who had been fed and rested. The two females, aunt and niece, were not informative. Deputy Trape was surprised at how gently bluff, heavyset Ep Lamister treated them. For himself, he was very impressed by the frail beauty of the younger woman, little more than a girl he would have said.

He was told that, during the stage-coach débâcle, she had fainted away. He wasn't surprised. The mess there was the worst he'd seen.

She was composed now, giving her name as Drusilla Bayley. She came from Chicago, as did her aunt, who preferred to be called Miss Lampett. She was plain, with an anxious manner.

But her niece, and ward, was another type of bird altogether, if as reticent, maybe shy. Golden hair, limpid blue eyes, a trim figure — what Denny could see of it — petite, vulnerable, so much so that Denny felt like taking her up in his arms, gently . . .

'C'mon, bucko,' said the sheriff. 'Let's go.' And they did, Ep grinning like a well-fed and knowing cat when they got outside the hotel. But he was dour and stern again when they met the two elderly business types and the weedy youth in the saloon.

The two older men weren't much help. The burlier and more outspoken of these two characters was still belly-aching about the way they'd been suckered — that was what he called it — into taking that particular stagecoach — and paying over the odds for the dubious privilege also.

Neither he or his partner, however, had much to add to what the law already knew, and that wasn't a lot.

Strangely, of the three male survivors of the murderous hold-up — those who had travelled first-class — the weedy youth was the most informative.

The two coach hackeys, sharing a table and eats and booze in another part of the large bar-room had talked themselves dry and were now taking things mighty easy. Their flamboyant equipage was out there in the main street with a cluster of folks of all ages inspecting it, though Tubs Smildey, who was standing sentinel there, wouldn't let them get too nosey or picky.

Denny had said he'd take his turn later and Tubs knew that Chief Ep would see that that genial young pup would do just as he was told. But, for the time, those two characters were listening with interest to the weedy youth who went by the name of Burt Youngman, not an inappropriate name at that.

* * *

'Merry days,' said Soddie Bill.

They were out of the badlands. They had filled their canteens at a waterhole.

41

They had crossed the river, which had refreshed them. They were dirty, bleary-eyed and still mighty jaded, but they were in Mexico now, out of reach of *Norte-Americano* law and, ahead of them, shimmering like a mirage in the mid-morning heat haze, was the town to which Pete Torlando was taking them. He had told Bill that it was called Rancho Juanita.

Bill, his good humour restored and his spirits almost disgustingly cock-a-hoop, said that that was a helluva name for a town and he couldn't see anything that looked like a rancho anyway.

Pete said, 'There used to be a ranch there, though I don't remember it, just the legend . . . '

'What legend?'

'I was gonna tell yuh, wasn't I? A Mex lived there. His wife was named Juanita. He named the place after her. They couldn't have kids, so I heard. The ranch was the thing. They'd do anything to make it bigger, greater. The don had an army of hardhats who

42

rustled an' robbed an' killed just to make him big, his holdings the widest and the greatest . . .'

'He was a bit like you an' me I guess, chief.'

'Goddamnit, will you just quit interrupting . . . Well, this'n got his come-uppance anyway. A mob attacked the place one night and fired it. There was a rumour then that it could have been *rurales* getting their job done, finishing him for good an' all 'cos he'd been like thorns in their asses for far too long. His boys fled. His wife and other folks in the hacienda were burned to death. He wasn't home, it wasn't known where he was. When he got back he couldn't do anything. Everything was finished. He turned away. It was thought he'd gone over the river and into the badlands you an' me have just crossed. He was never seen again.'

'We could've passed his bones,' Bill said. 'I suppose the town just grew. Nesters, huh?'

'Yeh. Just a settlement at first. But it

grew, an' some smartie dubbed it Rancho Juanita like it used to be and the name stuck and the place prospered. You can get anything here, *amigo*, including fleeced down to your skin if you don't watch your ass.'

'Do tell!'

'Yeh. American cattle-buyers come over here sometimes, y'know, thinking there's a rancho here. They're moneyed folk. They get fleeced all right, and sometimes they disappear off the earth entirely.'

'It figures,' said Soddie Bill.

The town was like a smaller model of the usual Mexican metropolis. It even had a square of sorts, but there were no pretty *señoritas* parading there under the watchful eyes of their *duennas*, no smart *caballeros* with flashing eyes paying their dues at more than arm's length. There were only a bunch of tough-looking oldsters with wary eyes, clustered around the rim of what looked like a fountain but seemed to be dry. There was something about the town: a look, a feeling.

The old men watched the new arrivals, until one of them spoke up, calling out to Pete Torlando by name and in a friendly fashion.

And Pete got down from his weary horse and one old man rose and shook Pete by his hand and, politely, the rest of the oldsters lowered their searching eyes.

Passing on, both men led their horses. Pete said, 'That was Lobo Sandoza. He's retired now.'

Bill said, 'I heard o' him. A bloodthirsty *bandido*.'

'Ain't they all?'

They went right through to the end of the street and pulled up at a two-storey frame-house which could have been a hotel but obviously wasn't. There was a water-trough by a hitching rack and they left their mounts.

They climbed on to a narrow veranda, the clatter of their bootheels wakening the silence, and passed through a swing-door into a sort of lobby. A woman came through to them, slim, tall, swarthy, not young any more but still handsome. She came to a halt and looked at them. Then she asked, 'Where's Stefan?'

Torlando said, 'He ain't with us, Maybella. He got caught with some stolen cattle. We don't rightly know what happened to him.'

'You should've found out.' She had a throaty voice and her dark eyes were hard.

'We will. We'll go back.'

Maybella and her paramour, Joey Danco, had picked Stefan up in the street during an ice-cold thunderstorm, and the woman, who'd never had a kid of her own, nursed him through pneumonia. After that, he'd run errands for Maybella's girls and, because of Joey Danco, nobody messed with him. Danco was an old saddle-pard of Pete Torlando's. Stefan had wanted to join Torlando and his boys and Danco had talked Maybella into letting him go.

Now Stefan lay in a cot in Doc Jock's

place in Canyon Pass and he had been clawed near to death. But the two outlaws and the handsome madam didn't know that part of the story.

Maybella, however, didn't like what she'd heard so far and she was voluble about that, even loud. Joey Danco came on to the scene and wanted to know what all the yelling was about. He was a quiet man with a hatchet face and strange pale eyes.

He greeted Pete Torlando like the friend Pete was, but not with the deference that might be accorded to the notorious gunfighting bandit leader. There was something about Danco's manner that was almighty challenging, the watching Bill thought, as Danco nodded to him, the newcomer, and did not take his hand.

7

When the weedy young man called Burt Youngman grinned his uneven teeth protruded and there was something mocking about his expression. He said, 'Nobody takes much notice of me.' And he grinned all the more. The hold-up débâcle was behind him and he was safe. He even seemed a mite cock-a-hoop. Ep Lamister, putting on his small-town lawman act, played him like a fish. And young Burt, though not exactly a mine of information, was somewhat smarter than he seemed, was quiet when he figured to be and watched and listened and cogitated.

It seemed to the watching and listening Denny, who wasn't much older than Burt, that the latter was, despite his lack of years, almost as cunning as the older man.

His family were Easterners with

money, his father a speculator who would speculate on almost anything he figured would make him a dollar or two. He had sent his son to explore this particular part of the West where, with civilization and the law moving in and getting stronger, there could be prime pickings. That was how Burt came to be in the border way-station, not far from a newly found gold-mine.

Burt had kept his eyes open. He had also kept his ears sharpened and he had listened to a feller called Dick Pedlar, who worked for the stage company, and some of his bosses, colleagues and cronies. He had heard about the gold shipment that was going up-country. He hadn't been able to find out where it was going, but, he, among all the passengers, was the only person who had learned how the gold was being sent and he had cut himself a piece of that.

Even now, talking to the sheriff, he couldn't explain why he had taken such a chance, he being a sort of weakling who had never had a gun in his hand let alone fired one.

But, once committed, his passage paid for on the trip in the special coach, he had gone along.

At the last moment the man called Dick Pedlar, who was supposed to be one of the guards — under the guise of being a passenger — had gotten a dose of croup and had taken to his bed. Another young man who had just happened to be in the vicinity had taken Dick's place for a high payment, him being a gunfighter like Dick and, supposedly, even better.

He was the one who had been killed during the hold-up by one of Torlando's men. He, it seemed, had not been quite good enough.

'You know Torlando?' Sheriff Lamister asked.

'I heard his name from your lips,' said Burt. 'But I had seen him before, just once. With Dick Pedlar.' And, out of earshot of Burt Youngman, the sheriff asked his deputy, 'Do you know who Dick Pedlar is?'

'How would I?' said Denny. 'Do you?'

'Jo-Jo MacTeen was a sort of cousin of Pedlar. He visited in the old days before he went further down to the border.'

'But if Jo-Jo was in cahoots with his cousin, or whatever, how come Jo-Jo got killed in the way he was and then was dumped on our doorstep?'

'I guess that's another mystery we have to solve,' said Ep Lamister.

They went to see Brazos Tom. He was still alive, but still possum-like also. They were surprised to find that the rustling younker who'd been clawed by a wildcat had his eyes open but was not right into the world, stared glassily, and mumbled, obviously unaware of what had happened to him. Still, Doc Jock had feared he might lose this particular patient who, the law hoped, might even be able to give them some information at a later date.

But they couldn't wait long. The

information they had got from Burt Youngman had been valuable. They knew that the notorious Pete Torlando was the one they had to be after — and whether the cat-clawed younker had had anything to do with Torlando or not was a question that might have to hang in the air for a long while.

★   ★   ★

Ep had some telegraphing to fix. Denny and he compared notes. All the big-coach hackeys had known where they were going but, of course, not what they were carrying. They, like the passengers, had thought that the trip, over the chosen rough trail, had been a test for the specially-built vehicle on its maiden voyage.

Their destination had been an ex-mining town, now a thriving though not large place — smaller than Canyon Pass — called Tarbuck after the prospector who'd found a small mine there which had since petered out.

There was decent rangeland around the settlement, however, so folks had stayed there, settled; stores had been built, a school, a church.

Tarbuck also had a telegraph office — similar to the one in Canyon Pass. It had a stage station, an assay office and, most notable of all, a bank that had the largest, strongest vault in that territory or for many miles around.

Ep said, 'I reckon it was gold not currency that that coach was carryin'. We know where it started from. There's a mine not a helluva way from there. The stuff could've been transported secretly, loaded secretly.'

'Somebody would have to know.'

'Yeh, that goes without sayin'. A chain, sort of, the first ending being the vault at Tarbuck. From there, later, to where? Who knows? Collections over time maybe . . . '

'The first place, the coach station, where is that, chief?'

'A place which is sometimes called Cottonwood Draw, or used to be. It has

53

no law, just a company settlement with some hard boys, a telegraph office. It's just a way-station. I guess nothing valuable has been transported from there before, wouldn't have been expected, not the place for it. Cunning, huh?'

'Cunning,' Deputy Denny agreed.

They got a posse together. Denny asked, 'What about Rancher Bogal?'

Ep said, 'He'll do what he figures he has to do I guess. As for us, we ain't got anybody to actually chase, so we might as well get a good night's sleep. Tell the boys. Top o' Main, first light, and anybody who can't make it gets left behind.'

Tubs Smildey was delegated to stay behind, watch the jail, to be the man packing the star for Canyon Pass. He made a token grumble but knew what his duty was. His son, Steve, would leave his gunshop in charge of an assistant and join his father as temporary deputy in case of need.

When the time came all the posse-members turned up, so there were seven in all, counting Denny and the sheriff. The latter was the elder and he carried his authority the way he always had, and they all knew his ways.

They took a last look at the strange coach that had been a sort of forerunner of all of this, made a few jocular remarks and then were on their way. The nearby hostler and his boys would be watching 'that contraption' and reporting to Deputy Smildey if anybody tried to interfere with the showy, unwieldylooking equipage.

★ ★ ★

Brazos Tom and the boy Stefan shared a small room in back of Doc Jock's place. A bed on each wall, a rush carpet in between them, a small table at the side of each narrow cot. Stefan spent most of his time sleeping now, not making noises any more, just breathing gently and regularly; good sign, Doc had said.

Brazos Tom had slept. Jock wasn't so

sure of him. His eyes had flickered and he had mumbled some, but he hadn't made any sense. Hell's bells, neither of them had. And the law had had to be on its way after the killing and robbing bandit gang.

Tubs Smildey was still around if anything new happened with the two patients, the two prisoners — if either of them talked sense at last, that was. And, if necessary, Tubs could try telegraphing the sheriff, if he could catch him; leaving a message at one place or another anyway.

Although nobody was aware of the fact, of course, Brazos Tom was one feller who knew something about what was going on. He drifted in and out of consciousness, spasms of grinding pain and then an almost stunning dullness. But in between times he played possum. And he listened.

His left-hand side was swathed in bandages and he knew that he would never use that arm again, had heard the old Doc say so. But he was a right-handed man and, though he figured (and hoped) that even the doc might figure him soon for worm-bait, he was in fact getting stronger.

He had already had his feet out of bed a couple of times when there was nobody else in the room but the sleeping Stefan. Maybe Stefan would die, Tom thought. He didn't figure the boy in on anything, so he didn't care one way or the other. Brazos Tom, cripple or not, figured still on a good right arm. And escape. And money. And maybe men to kill — men who might have left him to rot here otherwise.

As well as fighting and killing them, he had lived with Indians, with a Comanche squaw once for instance. Before meeting Pete Torlando he had run with the renegade polyglot *comancheros*, as cruel and ruthless as any Indian, and as hard, hating everybody but their own, thinking only of rape and pillage and booty, not fighting for freedom and prestige as many an

Indian — Comanche, Apache — whatever, might.

Brazos Tom had the endurance of any Comanche or Apache (those great guerrilla war-makers) but was without their tribal rules and customs . . .

And soon there was the night. And Tom's stockinged feet touched the floor once more and he found his boots under the bed, his clothing under the table beside the bed, stacked neatly — but, of course, no weapon.

He sat on the bed and gathered himself together, ignoring the gnawing at his shoulder — though it brought tears to his eyes. He put his clothes on slowly; oh, so slowly. He dragged his boots on and almost passed out. He wouldn't risk lying back again. He sat on the edge of the bed, fighting himself . . .

8

Maybella said, 'You've got to find out what's happened to Stefan.'

Soddie Bill said, 'He might be dead.'

Maybella erupted, her fine body shaking, her handsome face reddening. 'Damn your useless hides, both o' yuh. You've got to do something or, somehow, I'll make you pay, I swear.'

Bill backed a little. He'd never seen this woman like this before. But Pete Torlando stood his ground, said, 'We'll study on it.'

Bill had had a sudden thought, although it made his brain ache. 'If he's still in the land o' the living he might talk.'

Torlando snapped, 'What's he know?'

'He knows this place.' Bill was peeved at his chief. It wasn't Pete's way to act so stupid. Unless he had a reason for it of course. If he had in this case, Bill couldn't figure what it was. Hell, Stefan had been recruited here on the say-so of Pete's friend, Joey Danco, who may have had an ulterior motive; like getting the kid out of his hair for instance.

Maybella hadn't wanted that, but she'd been overruled by the two men and the kid himself. Now the woman was mighty worried about her 'chick'.

Bill thought Maybella wouldn't have had a caring bone in her whole handsome body ... However, he suddenly wanted to do what Maybella wanted.

Maybe Stefan would talk — if he was still alive. Maybe he'd lead folks here to Rancho Juanita.

Bill and Pete had the boodle. It was hidden now where nobody could find it. Maybella, and her man, cunning Joey Danco, would want to know. Fat chance! 'All right,' said Pete, nothing more. Bill wondered what Pete had up his sleeve.

But then the lean chief asked a question: 'Dick Pedlar here?'

'Haven't seen him yet,' said May-bella.

'Me neither,' said Joey Danco.

Time he was here if he wants his damn' cut, Soddie Bill reflected. But he didn't say anything.

★ ★ ★

Brazos Tom sat on the edge of the cot getting himself together while the darkness crept into the room between the gap in the curtains. Finally he hauled himself to his feet, steadied himself against a slight dizziness. This passed and he moved his feet, first one then the other, placing them carefully, moving forward like a drunken man striving to keep steady and half-way managing that.

He glanced from time to time at the boy in the other bed, just a dark shape not taking up much room, breathing gently but still as stone.

The door had been left open wide enough for Tom to insinuate himself carefully through.

He did not see the gleam of the boy Stefan's eyes open and stare at the door and then at the empty pallet opposite, the blankets thrown back. Tom could have made some sort of a dummy, covered. But that would have meant bending, stretching, and the man had not risked that, had just wanted to get away. Through the kitchen to the window which had been left open to let in the cooling breeze, such as it was. But Tom felt a slight exhilaration from it, pausing there.

He was padded and wrapped like an Egyptian mummy and, beneath all that, what had once been his left shoulder, of which there wasn't much left, nagged like a raging toothache.

There was a convenient wooden chair beneath the window and he hauled himself up on to its seat. He reached up, sweat pouring from him now, despite the breeze being more fully on his face. He managed to pull the window-sash down as far as it would go. He leaned on it, breathing heavily, drums beating in his head, his chest, spears digging at his shoulder. As if he were some kind of sacrifice.

He did not wait. He fought. He reached the sill with his feet. He hauled himself upwards once more.

Then, almost miraculously it seemed, he was through the window. *He was out.*

He let himself slide down against the wall to a sitting position. But he didn't stay there long . . . Cursing under his breath, he moved in the night. It was dark, with no moon. Pale stars winked high in the heavens. There was enough glow, however, for him to see his way through the shadowy backs of town, and no artificial lighting now. The night had been a long one and the darkness had come late, but no noise spilled from the back of the saloon and Tom went up the alley beside that establishment and on to the quiet main street.

He found himself opposite the strange, long stagecoach that had been his target earlier and, because of a shot-gun toting stage-guard who hadn't lived to tell the tale, had brought Brazos Tom to this parlous position.

He skirted the vehicle and came out in front of the dark stables. He went up the narrow, uneven alley at the side and round to the narrow back door and a window which was slightly open. First of all he tried the door, was surprised to find it unlocked. In this town folks obviously still trusted their neighbours.

He opened the door, slid through and leaned against the wall beside it. Begod, he needed the rest anyway! He stood with his head bowed on his chest and listened. Slight sounds, probably from the horses in the front part of the building. The stagecoach nags, and others. He had to get through to there. Get some kind of a weapon also, if he could find one.

He raised his head, tried to peer through the darkness, dispel some of it with his fevered gaze.

Slowly, he saw images. He was in a

kitchen. To the right of him was a communicating door to another place. This door was slightly open. He dragged himself across to it. Then he heard the snoring coming from the other side of the door.

He opened the door a little wider and peered in.

A window sparsely curtained. A bed from which the snoring issued. Bits of furniture that didn't look much. He saw something gleaming in a corner that was quite near to him. A familiar shape — although he could hardly believe that the luck was still running so well for him.

In a moment he had reached the weapon, captured, backed, was once more in the kitchen.

Behind him, the snoring continued without a break.

He was outside. He closed the door gently behind him. Now he had to get back to the front of the place, hoping it was as easy to get in there as it had been in the back. The Winchester rifle was loaded. Now he had to get a horse, maybe even a saddle. A saddle-blanket anyway. He had to sit on something. He was used to being on horseback. He could even rest like that. He felt that if he didn't rest in some way he was likely to fall to pieces and turn finally to dust.

★ ★ ★

The Teller brothers were thieves. They were harmless, but they were thieves, had always been thieves. Their father had been a thief, but he'd stolen horses and had been caught and hanged by a bunch of vigilantes. Their mother had run off with a whiskey drummer. Their sister was a whore in San Antone.

The brothers weren't aiming to go the way of the rest of the family. Anyway, they preferred to stay at home — but they'd filch anything that wasn't too big (like horses or cattle) and wasn't nailed down.

All day they'd been surreptitiously eyeing the ornate stagecoach. After leaving the saloon they'd hung around in hiding. Then, when everybody else had gone home, they'd approached the silent vehicle that loomed in the night. There'd surely be something worth lifting from there. The night was their thing anyway and, like cats in the dark, they were filled with an insatiable curiosity.

They knew that the old hostler Ben had kept an eye on the coach during the day. But they had seen Ben leaving the saloon, staggering like he'd been hit in the head by a two-by-four. Ben would be no trouble. If you wanted a horse in the night you'd need to blow an army bugle in the ear of that old souse. His boy, Dick, was no better a watcher by night. Ben had said himself that 'that boy' slept like he never wanted to wake and was almighty hell to rouse come morning.

So — as it happened — the Teller brothers were coming down from the long stagecoach with items that other folk might term inconsidered trifles — though the boys would no doubt find some use for them — when they saw the feller come out of the stables leading a horse with a saddle-blanket over its back.

Brazos Tom had been mighty quiet. He was as surprised to see the two night-birds as they were to see him. With his good right arm he was leading the horse by a hackamore which hadn't been hard to find, that and a saddle-blanket but no actual saddle. He managed to tote the rifle also in his right hand.

One of the boys said, 'Hey!' He was the younger one and as harmless as a newborn kitten. The other one got nervous, though, and reached for his gun. But, no more than his brother, he was no hammer-slammer.

Brazos Tom had used a rifle one-handed before. On horseback. He raised it but little higher than his waist and pressed the trigger. The slug hit the elder brother full in the chest and he went over as if he'd been kicked.

The younger boy wailed like a stricken animal. He seemed as if he would throw himself upon his brother's still body. But he thought better of it and dived for cover around the corner of the stagecoach.

A weakness had come over Brazos Tom once more. He managed to haul himself up on the stolen horse, holding grimly to the hackamore — and the rifle — and drum his heels into the beast's flanks. The horse had been startled by the gun going off in his ear, was ready to go — and did.

The younger brother hauled out his old Colt and took a shot at the fleeing rider, missing by a small mile.

The younger brother crawled to his dead kin, was holding his brother's head in his arms and crooning sorrowfully to the dead face as the townsfolk began to gather by.

Among them was Doc Jock, who said that young Stefan, who had shared a sickroom with Brazos Tom, had told him of the wounded man's escape.

'I should've got here sooner.'

'If you had he might've shot you as well,' said Deputy Tubs, there with his son.

'He'll maybe kill himself anyway,' said the doc. 'He shouldn't even be out of bed.' He bent to the younger Teller. 'C'mon, son. I can't do anything for your brother. I'm almighty sorry.'

The old hostler and his son brought out the horses of the two deputies. The genial drunk and snoozy offspring were both wide awake now and doing all they could. Undertaker Dickie Moley came forth, his the last melancholy task.

★ ★ ★

Sheriff Ep Lamister and his boys reached the place they sought, Cottonwood Draw, finding it in a state of flux. Everybody seemed to know now that money was missing. Boodle anyway,

70

though some didn't know what form it took.

The sheriff asked about Dick Pedlar, the man who at the last moment hadn't been able to travel with the handsome stagecoach because he had an attack of croup.

Dick it seemed had speedily gotten over his illness and had left town.

Somebody said he had gone 'borderways'.

The sheriff didn't seem too surprised at any of this news and, after taking a quick bite and a drink apiece, he and his boys went on their way. They were manhunters now, pure and simple, and they sure as hell were not returning yet to Canyon Pass.

They had had information from the weedy coach passenger called Burt Youngman, now taking it easy in Canyon Pass — at least that was what was figured — and Sheriff Lamister seemed to know where he was going.

The boys, refreshed after their short rest and sustenance, their mounts raring to go, followed their leader willingly, though even Ep's deputy, Denny Trape, didn't seem to rightly know what the big feller was up to. And they crossed the river.

9

Deputy Tubs Smildey and his son, Steve, left Canyon Pass, following the direction Brazos Tom had taken. This trail led past the frame-house where Tubs lived with his wife, Steve's mother, Dulcie. Out here on the edge of town habitations were spaced further apart but the Smildeys' neighbours weren't too far away; this was a very neighbourly off-shoot community.

Young Steve and his wife lived at the gunshop which they ran with great expertise.

Lights were flashing in windows before the two riders came upon Tub's place.

'Something's up,' said Tubs in alarm.

A man ran out at them, shouting. Tubs, who was nearest to the neighbour, went on, 'Seems like that skunk's holed-up.'

They drew up outside Tubs's place where two more men were crouching with guns drawn. Faintly, as they reined in, they could hear the thud of a horse's hooves. The sound died.

One of the men said, 'He fell off the hoss here an' Dulcie ran out to help him. He ran her into the house with a rifle.'

Tubs and Steve dismounted. 'Stay down, boys,' the older man said. 'Cover us.'

As the man and his son, guns out, approached the frame-house with the wide veranda, one front window lit up there, a gun spoke. But the shot was wide, passing between the two men as they advanced, drawing wider apart.

A rough, shaky voice yelled, 'I've got the woman here. If you don't back off I'll kill her.'

The two men exchanged glances, sank on their bellies.

His hand low, brushing the grass, Tubs made a signal to his son. Steve, wriggling like a snake, keeping as low as he could, moved further away from his father, making for the side of the house.

'I'll kill her,' the voice called again, sounding kind of crazy. Steve became still. But he was nearer to the corner of the veranda. He stayed put, though, as his father signalled to him again.

★   ★   ★

Dulcie Smildey was a handsome woman as tall as her tubby swain. She had curly red hair touched with grey, and green eyes that looked straight at you. She had been a young beauty. Now she was a mature one. She had never been a simpering missy. She was a staunch frontierswoman whose husband was a lawman and she had stood by him in the good times and the bad. All in all, their lives together had been pretty good in any way you could mention. She still had her good figure, her healthy body and, as she herself had throatily put it, her 'Tubs' was still no slouch. They still had some good bed-times together.

She looked at the man in front of her, the man she had tried to help when the reckless horse had thrown him and galloped onwards. She had since realized who the man was. A wounded killer who wasn't worthy of her help, or of anybody else's.

He sat on the battered *chaise-longue* which was Tubs' favourite when he wanted to put his feet up. His blood was staining the flowered fabric. He pointed his rifle at her, the stock slick with blood. The fall from the horse had obviously opened his wound again. Tubs had told her that it was a terrible one.

How had this man even got this far?

He was pointing his rifle at her, but the muzzle was slowly lowering. His eyes had been like the eyes of a crazed animal in the last agonizing throes of its existence. The lids drooped, and then they shot upwards again, only to droop once more. His shouting had obviously tired him. She didn't think he'd be able to shout again.

She said, 'You need help very badly. I wanted to help you. I can't help you. You need Doc Jock who helped you before. It's his job and he'll do it even for you as he already has. You were foolish to run away. If you try anything else you're surely going to die.'

It was as if she was talking to a rough, misbehaving child.

'You'll die first,' he mumbled.

She hardly caught the words.

The muzzle of the rifle lifted. She braced herself to move. To move with great rapidity. But the rifle-muzzle dropped. Lower. Lower . . .

He wasn't looking at her any more. There seemed to be a glaze over his eyes, hideous in the lamplight. The eyes closed. The rifle fell, hit the floor, and the man followed it, landing in a bundle at her feet, his blood staining the rough rush carpeting. The hideous wounded shoulder was hidden, though, and so was the face.

Dulcie did not have to bend over the body in order to make sure he was dead. This bundle did not even look like a man any more, just a dead *thing*.

She was suddenly weary, but she rose.

As she often did, she had been sitting at the window here in the place they called 'The living room', looking out, hoping that Tubs would be able to come in quickly for a cup of coffee, maybe a bite, while Steve looked after the law office for him.

She had had the curtains half-drawn back. She had heard the galloping horse, a wild sound. She had seen the rider falling and had run out — to be greeted by a hurting, half-crazy man who had pushed a rifle-barrel into her face and made her do what he said.

Now she went to the door, opened it, stepped out on to the veranda, called the men in.

Doc Jock turned up, looked down at his late patient, said, 'Obviously he wasn't as tough as he thought he was.'

Dick Pedlar had arrived in Rancho Juanita and Pete Torlando had said to him, 'We're gonna try an' find out what happened to young Stefan and you're coming with us.'

Pedlar protested, 'My cousin Jo-Jo is dead and I heard one of yours did that, not one o' the others.'

'Brazos Jack did it,' Torlando said. 'He figured that Jo-Jo was gonna run to his old friends in the law, get back in favour, get a reward.'

'Jo-Jo wouldn't have done that.'

'Too late to argue about that now.'

'You acted on my say-so. It ain't my fault everything didn't go as planned. But you got the stuff, didn't you? I want my cut, and then . . . '

'You get no cut till we get back,' said Torlando.

'That's right,' said Soddie Bill, standing at his chief's side.

Torlando went on, 'If we don't do like I say we're gonna have trouble with

Maybella, and we don't want that, do we? She's been a good friend to us for a long time and she sure as hell has more friends as well in this neck of the woods than we'll ever have. She's been a great help. She wants her boy back and, if he's to be got, we'll get him, there's no argument about that. Oh, I tried, yeh, but f'Chrissakes, you know Maybella as well as we do!'

It wasn't like the chief to do so much explaining, Bill thought, particularly to a long streak of urine like Dick Pedlar, whether he'd been useful or not — and he had. But now maybe Pete had something in mind for Dick and the ride out would be the start of it.

And ride out they did, the three of them. A hell of a chance, thought Bill. Back over the river to where the North-American lawmen prowled. And him and Torlando already with prices on their head, and more now no doubt. The only consolation was that the Anglo law wouldn't be expecting them back.

But all for the sake of a snot-nosed kid who might be dead anyway, and a crazy whore who wanted her child back, it seemed, more than she wanted the pickings that would accrue to her, if and when the rescuers got back, with or without her precious Stefan.

10

The posse approached Rancho Juanita by night and, outside the settlement, they split up. Sheriff Lamister led three men off the main trail. Deputy Denny Trape led the others round back and came in the other end of the little peculiarly named town.

Once in the town, Ep sent his three men in different directions. Two of them knew Pete Torlando by sight. One of them didn't, but he knew Soddie Bill and it was figured that that small scruffy outlaw was now Torlando's companion. There could be others as well, of course: who knew?

They knew where to find their chief if they wanted him. Otherwise they were to keep away from the main saloon, the cantinas, rathskellars and other dives of which Rancho Juanita had a bewildering variety.

They were not actually to meet the other bunch, at first to ignore them if they came in their sight. Denny and his boys would do the same. And, barring incidents, they all knew where to meet their chief at a given time.

Ep Lamister had gone to visit his old friend, though not an ally, Maybella. That madam would never be an ally of the law, but Ep was a tolerant man, as most good lawmen tended to be in the polyglot South-west, particularly the border regions. Ep was way out of his bailiwick anyway, didn't carry any authority in Rancho Juanita at all. It might be said that right now he needed a friend in that town.

He wondered whether Joey Danco was still with Maybella, was disappointed to learn that he was. Still, as far as Ep knew, there was no price yet on that hatchet-faced gunfighter's head. Anyway, even if there was, Ep couldn't do anything about it, didn't particularly want to as long as Joey sang small, as he was cunning enough to do: he had a good thing going with the richest madam in this territory . . .

Ep had known Maybella when she was one of the girls in an establishment in El Paso and he was a fledgling lawman just making his mark, a handsome young man who had the knack of getting on with anybody, particularly those of the female gender.

He had had some good times with Maybella before he moved on to better things, to top lawman in Canyon Pass, going back to the town he'd known as a kid and to old friends, going back to marriage with an old schoolmate and to the sadness that had followed that. But staying. And hearing now and then news about Maybella, who had gone on to greater things . . .

In between times he met Maybella once when she was on a shopping expedition back in El Paso and they were both visiting old friends. Ep was a widower by then, but nothing had come out of the chance meeting with Maybella who, like most madams, had her 'protector' with her, Joey Danco; and, strange though it might seem to Ep, or anybody else, the elegant ex-chippie was mighty fond of the young man. Yeh, Joey, who could be said to have the lean, fine looks and rough charm that had been Ep's great assets in the old days.

Now, in Rancho Juanita, Joey greeted Ep with a poker face which wore no hint of surprise and didn't turn a dark hair when Maybella flung her arms about an old friend and gave him a smacking kiss, though that gesture had no lust about it whatsoever.

So Ep got a pretty good welcome. But no information. Maybella didn't claim to have no knowledge of Pete Torlando but said she didn't know where he was now. And that could be the truth.

The bordello had a palatial dining area and there Ep's boys joined him. They weren't allowed to dally with any of the girls, much though some of them might have welcomed such a delicious break. Though even sworn-in Anglo deputies had no jurisdiction whatsoever in old Mexico, they were, as they saw it, still on duty and had no time for dilly-dallying.

They had done the town. Oh, Pete Torlando and Soddie Bill had been here all right, but they weren't here any more and nobody knew where they were now.

Then Ep Lamister had a stroke of luck.

In the plaza in the centre of the little town he was greeted by another old friend.

Although he did not know it, this friend was the same man who had earlier spoken to Pete Torlando when that bandit leader had ridden in with his scruffy companion. An old *bandido* who had been even more notorious than Torlando was now. Lobo Sandoza, retired. He told Ep Lamister which way Torlando had gone, something the North-American lawman was unable to figure — unless the old man was just plainly jealous of the young Anglo upstart who was getting as famous

— and in Mexico too — as Lobo himself had once been.

They found a general stores by the river and they got more information. The two riders, as described, had gone back over the river.

Ep Lamister said, 'What the hell . . . ?'

* * *

Rancher Simon Bogal was a cantankerous, dogmatic, single-minded old jasper, but he was willing to admit, if only to himself, when he'd pulled a boner.

Even with the help of that ace-high Indian tracker, Silencio, he could not figure out the trail the two outlaws had taken across the badlands. So he and the boys — including Silencio this time — had to turn back again. Anyway, they'd got the cattle back, hadn't they, all of 'em?

The bunch went back home.

Maybe the law would come up with something . . .

Some of the boys had off-time coming to them now. They went on into Canyon Pass.

There were four of them. Four cowboys, glad to get away from hard ground and rocks that reflected the sun in a blinding way. Glad to get away from stunted vegetation, food for neither man nor beast, bitter poison weed. And nothing ahead but the same for countless miles, and an atmosphere that choked a man. Hell, a man could die in those badlands and lie till he was bones; and then dust dissipating them in a treacherous breeze that had no cooling powers at all.

Two men seemed to have got away across there. Two rustlers. But maybe they hadn't . . . But, anyway, it was best to forget. There was a spree ahead. The four boys were on the main trail to town and soon town would come into sight under a sun that wasn't as hot as it had been, though maybe that was only their imaginations playing them tricks. Ugh, those badlands!

Three horsemen passed across the trail in front of them, not aiming for Canyon Pass it seemed, skirting it, going someplace else. Their three faces were lit momentarily by the sun and then they were on their way, horsemen's backs, steeds' wagging rumps receding into the distance.

But, staring after the trio, one of the four cowboys grabbed his companion by the arm, asked, 'See them?'

'Sure I see'd them. So?'

'Them are the two rustlers you an' me spotted when we found the beef an' that young gink and the dead wildcat.'

'There are three of 'em,' said the other man stupidly. The other two members of the quartet stared at the arguing pair. Still, they were old-time pards and they were always arguing about something or other.

The dogmatic one said, 'I don't know the other feller. But that's the two I mentioned.'

'Nah, can't be,' scoffed his friend. 'Why would they come back here?

They'd be crazy to come back here, wouldn't they?'

For the first time the dogmatic one looked doubtful. 'I guess . . .'

'And where would they be goin' anyway?' his friend asked. 'C'mon, bucko, you've mebbe got a touch o' the sun. You need a drink, you shorely do.'

'Well . . .' Still doubtful.

The four went on their way and soon entered the convivial town of Canyon Pass and the big saloon.

When the dogmatic cowboy first joined the crew of the Cross Kettle Ranch he had been dubbed 'Pug', short for pugilist, which was what he'd been since his early youth, a member of one of the boxing teams that roamed the West, bare-knuckle, catch-as-catch-can Pug had busted the knuckles on his left hand pretty badly. He was finished as a brawler — and he'd been a good one. He didn't mind cowpunching, though, admitted that it was as congenial, and a damn' sight less hurting, than his other profession had been.

He was a quick learner, busted hand or not, still had his good right mitt. He was stocky, with a broad chest and lots of muscle. But he was fast also, with rope, with gun, with branding iron and stirrups.

He was a man who had always kept himself fit and his still young face was comparatively unmarked except for a bent nose that gave him a genial, roguish look. He wasn't a man you could mess with.

As he and his three saddle-pards entered the saloon Pug seemed to have forgotten about the three strangers they had spotted, two of whom he had affirmed were not exactly strangers at all.

Back at the ranch Pug still did what he called callisthenics. Tying himself in damn' knots, his friend Tocky always said. And, true to his good health regime, Pug did not imbibe a lot of strong drink, said it went right to his head in fact.

But, after their dry sojourn in the badlands, their escape from there you might say, the boys were in the mood for celebrations, and, joining in the spirit of things, Pug bent more than usual, tried to keep up with the others.

They sat at a table in a window overlooking the main street. The sun's ray slanted past them and they could, if the fancy took them, look out on the passing throng. The sun wasn't as powerful as it had been and the work-a-day tasks of most folk were almost finished with. The saloon began to fill up.

The four boys became cheerful and rowdy, and Pug was no exception. They made comical remarks about people they saw pass by outside.

Suddenly Pug's expression became hard, fixed, as he gazed at something outside. He rose to his feet. 'It's them two again,' he said. 'Not the other one this time, just them two. I'd know 'em anywhere.' Before any of his friends could expostulate with him, he made for the batwings.

11

Denny Trape said, 'Maybe we could've passed 'em on the way goin' in when they were coming out.'

The sheriff said, 'I didn't see any horsemen who'd made me look again. Did you?'

'I guess not.'

'They wouldn't have taken this main trail either way I don't think. Not those boys. Not that cunning fox, Torlando. He'd have his own ways.'

'I guess you're right, chief. But why would they be going back anyway?' Denny gave a little humourless laugh. 'Did they leave somep'n behind, d'you think?'

'I've been cogitatin' on that. They left Brazos Tom behind. And I'm also beginning to wonder whether that wounded rustler kid who got clawed by the wildcat was part of that bunch also.'

93

'Neither of them have been able to talk.'

'If they survive maybe they will. Torlando would want their mouths shut for good.'

'More boodle for him an' the other feller, huh?'

'Likely,' said Sheriff Ep Lamister.

'You didn't get much outa that madam, did you?' said Deputy Trape.

The other boys were looking at them curiously. Going back without anything after their long ride didn't sit with them too well. And now the two principals seemed to be arguing, if not in a too unfriendly way.

Ep answered Denny's question in an oblique way. 'Me an' Maybella don't see eye to eye much nowadays I guess.'

Unspeaking now, Denny thought about Maybella's man, Joey Danco, whom he'd met for the first time. He'd taken a violent dislike to the man. A snake with killer's eyes. Maybe if they could've got that one on his own and worked on him . . .

But that hadn't seemed possible. Now Denny felt a small let-down, wondered what they were going into now — if anything! And their horses' hooves ate up the miles.

★ ★ ★

The other three boys followed Pug from the saloon, but when they got out into the fading sunshine, they couldn't see him anywhere. It was as if he'd gone to ground like a gopher.

'The alley,' said Pug's friend, Tocky, after they had gone back and forth, peering like brainless chickens.

Tocky turned into the alley beside the saloon, peeved with himself because he hadn't thought of that right off. The alley was empty. At the other end the sun slanted in.

With the other two boys behind him, he went up the narrow passage. The ground was mighty uneven and littered with miscellaneous rubbish. The three men moved clumsily on high-heeled

95

riding boots. Tocky stumbled and the man behind cannoned into him.

'Dammit, get off me!' But Tocky reached the end of the alley and peered round the corner. *Nothing*.

* * *

Dick Pedlar was not a wanted man. He wasn't known in Canyon Pass either. He wanted Brazos Tom. Tom had killed his cousin, Jo-Jo, Pete Torlando had told Dick so. Dick wanted revenge: it was a family thing. He separated himself from Pete and Bill. Torlando didn't object to this: Bill and he had to keep out of sight as much as possible.

It was Pedlar who found out that Brazos Tom was already dead, his shattered body lying in the undertaking parlour. Pedlar also learned that the boy Stefan still lay in the doctor's surgery, from which Brazos Tom had escaped only to die miserably in a house on the trail, his wounds and his over-taxed heart getting the better of him.

Pedlar and the two other men had arranged to meet in a disused feed-shed they'd found behind the livery stables. When Pedlar got there at the allotted time Torlando and Soddie Bill were nowhere in sight. Pedlar waited, looking at his Eastern-made small pocket-watch from time to time.

He had heard that young Stefan was still alive, mending even. They had to get the boy away. That was what they had come here for, wasn't it? Torlando and Bill wouldn't have taken the risk otherwise. Did they mean to kill the boy to keep his mouth shut — despite what they'd promised Maybella, tell her some horse-shit story maybe about the boy already being dead?

Where were the boys anyway? Had they some deep-laid scheme to cut him out altogether?

★　★　★

Pug came face to face with the two men he sought, and then more than ever he

97

was sure that these were the rustlers that Tocky and he had seen on the edge of the dip by the badlands. The two who had escaped through the badlands! He did not ask himself again what they might be doing here. He challenged them.

'I want to talk to you two gents,' he said.

The words were mundane. But this stocky feller's attitude — this powerful-looking young man with the crooked nose — was not friendly and the two outlaws had never seen him before. And Soddie Bill, for one, was getting kind of jittery, and he did the worst thing he could have done. He went for his gun.

He had never been a particularly fast draw. Not nearly so fast as Torlando or Brazos Tom for instance. He had the weapon only half out of its holster when Pug shot him in the chest.

At such close quarters, the heavy slug bored into him like a powerfully wielded Indian lance, went right through his body and out the other side, bringing with it a gout of blood and bone. Then he hit the ground hard, his legs kicking up and then stretching out, and he was as straight and still as if laid out for burial, Soddie Bill already returned to the earth.

'Raise 'em,' said Pug, jerking the gun in Torlando's direction.

Lightning draw or not, the lean outlaw didn't try it. He raised his paws, dutifully. But that was when the unforeseen happened.

Pug's three pards came running up behind him. Thinking he was being attacked from behind, maybe by some more of the outlaw gang, Pug half-turned.

Torlando brought one of the uplifted arms down, the fist at the end of it like a hammer. It caught Pug on his cheekbone, cracking it. The young man went down as if pole-axed, his gun flying from his hand.

Torlando didn't try gunplay, not against three strangers with blood in their eyes. He ran. He whipped around a corner.

He heard sounds of pursuit, figured

from the boot-heels that there were two men after him, the third looking after the bastard who had killed Bill.

Such was the case; Tocky was helping the dazed Pug to his feet, blood streaming down Pug's face. Pug bent, groping for his gun, almost fell over again. Tocky retrieved the Colt, stuck it in his friend's holster.

'You got one of 'em then?'

'He tried to throw down on me,' said Pug thickly.

Doc Jock appeared, undertaker Dickie Moley not far behind him. Those two were getting to be like bird dogs.

Tubs Smildey appeared, glanced at the body. 'Soddie Bill,' he said.

Doc Jock caught Pug's arm, said, 'C'mon, I've got to try and fix that face before it goes all lopsided on you.'

Everybody sort of whirled about as the two friends of Pug and Tocky appeared, breathing hard. One said, 'The other sonofabitch seems to have disappeared!'

Although none of the mystified

company knew this, by that time Pete Torlando had reached the disused feed-hut where Dick Pedlar awaited him.

Pedlar, risking the outlaw leader's wrath, demanded, 'Where've you been? And where's Bill?' Then: 'I thought I heard some shooting.'

'Bill's dead, and we've gotta get out of here for a while.'

They went through the back of the livery stables. Pedlar said, 'Brazos Tom's dead as well. But Stefan's still in the land of the livin'. And mending it seems.'

'Maybella will be pleased,' said Torlando sardonically. 'But the little scut will have to stay here now. We've got to get back. I'll handle that damn' madam.'

12

They didn't make any detour. They hit the main trail and they hit it hard.

They had no means of knowing that the returning Canyon Pass posse would be on the main trail, coming home.

The posse heard the sound of the madly galloping hooves. At that point, there were rock outcrops each side of the trail. At Sheriff Lamister's instructions, they split up into two sides. There was enough cover to take their horses too.

When the two riders came abreast in the dying sun, the sheriff shouted, 'Stop right there! There are seven guns pointing at you.'

The two men reined in, their horses' hooves skidding on the hard ground. The members of the posse came out. Torlando said something obscene but raised his hands above his head when

told to do that, his companion following suit.

The news was soon all around
town. The posse had brought two
hardcases in. Another was already dead,
laid out in young Dickie Moley's
body-parlour. There'd been a third
earlier, the wounded madman called
Brazos Tom . . . there was talk that the
cat-clawed younker who Doc Jock said
was called Stefan was an outlaw of
some sort, a rustler at least. Nobody
worried about him, though. Some of
the goodwives were sorry for him, took
him cakes and pies, in which the old
doc shared, surely.

The doc said his patient was a
healthy young cuss really. His wounds
had healed well. He would have to walk
with a stick for a longish while and,
even after that, might always have a
limp. But ribald speculations made by
godforsaken cowboys could be ignored,
Jock said: the rest of Stefan's equip-
ment should be all right.

Canyon Pass was suddenly besieged

by folks from all points of the compass. Some of them called themselves lawmen, some even 'government men', whatever that meant. There were a couple of Pinkertons who called themselves range detectives, two odd bounty-hunters who didn't seem to be doing anything in particular now Torlando was incarcerated. There were folks who called themselves 'agents' and some who referred to themselves as 'representatives'.

Representatives from Tarbuck which had the biggest bank vault in the territory, a vault that had been kept waiting, empty, and still was. They came from the other end of the line, Cottonwood Draw and the way-station where the boodle had been packaged in the long coach. They came like vultures from all over the place.

Sheriff Ep Lamister greeted them all with a sort of brusque courtesy which changed to a taciturn manner that seemed to border on stupidity, though this didn't fool anybody who had any common intelligence. But some of them hadn't — and two of those were hard boys who said they were from Cotton-wood Draw, near to the company mining area from which the boodle had come in the first place.

It was daylight. Tubs Smildey was on patrol and Ep and Denny were taking a rest in the jail office. The two cells at the back were empty. There were more bodies in the undertaking parlour and buryings would have to be fixed soon as Dickie Moley was running out of ice.

The two visitors came in without knocking. They were big men in broadcloth suits and, at first glance, might even have been taken for cattle-buyers. But there was another look about them which Denny (who'd been well-trained by his chief) picked up immediately — particularly as one of them drew a gun! He evidently wasn't the talker, though. It was the other one who said, 'We want no shilly-shallying. We want answers and we want 'em quick.'

Ep said, 'What in hell are you talkin'
about?'

'We think the hold-up was a set-up.
We think the loot is still around
someplace.' The talker had a black
moustache and sounded like an East-
erner. His companion was of about the
same size but clean-shaven, kind of
stupid-looking.

But the big Colt in his fist was as
steady as it could possibly be and the
cold eyes above it were implacable.

Ep said, 'Me an' my deputy have
been back an' forth like two blue-assed
buzzards an' we ain't got even a smell
of any loot.' The big man — although
he wasn't as big as either of the two
visitors — jerked a thumb in the
direction of his deputy who said,
'That's right.'

'Quit waving your arms about. Raise
'em above your heads and come out
from behind that desk.'

They did as they were told, and the
talker continued, with a question,
'Where are the two prisoners?'

Ep said, 'Where you'd expect them to be. In the cells in back.'

But the sheriff had been cuter than that. Torlando and Pedlar were, in fact, incarcerated in a root cellar under an eating-house a few doors away. The proprietor was an old friend, an ex-member of the posse. His hatch was battened down and there were two other ex-deputies on watch all the time. The three of them were as close-mouthed as if their lips had been sewn.

It had seemed to Ep that too many visiting folks wanted words with the outlaw pair. He had put the word out that Torlando and Pedlar had already been sent up-country for safer keeping and a trial. Evidently these two newcomers hadn't got that word.

Ep let Denny lead the way, following the younger man himself with the gun-toter right behind and the talker bringing up the rear. The feller with the Colt hadn't yet said a word, didn't seem as if he was going to.

Ep went through the communicating

door to the cell block. The door had been left slightly ajar and the sheriff only had to push it with the toe of his boot. It was well-oiled. It slid wide, swiftly.

Ep stopped dead in the narrow passage, the two empty cells ahead of him.

'Godamighty!' he exploded, rocking back on his heels. He was taking the devil's own chance and knew it — but it worked.

The stupid one with the steady gun suddenly wasn't steady any more, said, 'What . . .?' backed. Then Ep stepped to one side without turning, and his driving elbow hit the gun-toter in the belly with malignant force. The man went 'Oof' and doubled. His gun went off. The slug brushed Ep's pants leg at the hip. The report in the enclosed space was like a thunder-clap and the slug whined into one of the empty cells and thunked into a back wall.

Denny had had some idea of what his chief had planned to do. He knew that the man behind him would react, and he turned just as that big individual was reaching for his weapon which was in a shoulder holster inside his coat. He wasn't fast enough.

Deputy Denny was very fast, whirling, his knee rising, digging powerfully into the groin of the big feller who fell like a log but didn't stay that way. He writhed like his companion was doing on the floor nearby.

Both lawmen soon had guns in their hands, Denny hefting the weapon loosened from its owner's shoulder holster: a silvery, ivory-handled pistol the make of which he didn't recognize.

'Fancy!'

Tubs Smildey, who must have been nearby in the street, came butting in, gun in hand, stopped dead.

'Help us get these two jaspers in a cell apiece,' Ep said.

This was soon done. The three lawmen went back to the desk. Ep's and Denny's gun-rigs were on a spare chair near there. Ep picked his up and strapped it on, said, 'I guess we ought to tote these all the time, bucko.'

'I guess,' said Denny and followed his chief's example.

Ep said to Tubs, 'Look outside, make sure nobody's bin too alarmed by that shot.'

Tubs did this. They heard him talking, another voice or three. He came back. 'It's all right. I'll go finish my rounds. You boys keep outa trouble now, y'hear?'

The next visitor was Rancher Simon Bogal and he had a stocky young Pug in tow, swollen-jawed, kind of sheepish-looking too.

'You need any help, Ep?'

'Things are all right so far, Simon, thanks.'

'I'll leave some of my boys in town anyway. Pug thinks he ought to see you.'

Ep looked at the cowpuncher. 'That's good — but there was no need. Tubs told me the rights of it. Pug acted in self-defence. He bagged himself an outlaw. There could be a reward. I'll check.'

'Thankee, Mr Lamister.'

'Go back to the other boys, son.' And, as Pug left, Simon turned again to Ep. 'How about that other two? You keeping 'em here?'

'Sure. Until the circuit judge comes along. I've sent a hurry-up telegraph.'

'All right. I'm with you there, Ep.' Rancher Bogal took his leave.

The two prisoners in the cells began to shout. Denny went and told them if they didn't shut their faces he'd go fetch a bucket o' soapsuds and water 'em down.

13

Stefan sat up in bed, thinking hard. He reflected how decent the folks in this town had been to him, those he'd met that is, the visiting ones, the ladies with their gifts. And even the sheriff and his two deputies had been fair to a wounded boy who'd been picked up on a rustling charge. The plump, older deputy called Tubs — why, his handsome wife had even brought Stefan some fine cookies. Then, most of all, there was the doc. The consensus was it seemed that Doc Jock, held in affection by all the town, had saved Stefan's life.

What could Stefan do now, though? He was in a terrible quandary. He knew that Pete Torlando and that man, Pedlar, had been captured.

He didn't care about Pedlar.

But Pete was family.

Pete was family like Maybella was family, and even Joey Danco, who went along with Maybella on most things but had spoken on Stefan's behalf to his friend, Pete. And hadn't Maybella and Joey saved Stefan from dying in the gutter long before everything else happened?

You had to stick with family, Stefan thought. You had to do something! What might happen to him anyway? Would he be charged with Torlando and Pedlar? Would he go to jail?

He had seen Brazos Tom get out of that cot opposite. He had hated Tom and, to the doc, had blown the bugle on him. Now Tom was dead meat and Stefan wasn't going to bother his head about that. But Tom had sort of pointed the way, had got out through a kitchen, Stefan had heard that: it was something to toy with.

He was mending. He could go about this room with the stick Doc Jock had given him. His limp was pretty bad but he had practised and he was getting better at using the stick. Hell, he just had to do *something* . . .

* * *

The Canyon Pass folk were getting used to funerals. There had been as many in the last few days, less than a week, as there'd been for a twelve-month period before.

This was the morning for the burying of the older Teller brother, whose name was Ike (the younger brother was Clay), the notorious Brazos Tom, and another outlaw whose moniker Clay didn't know.

The folk who'd come to grief in the stagecoach hold-up had been buried earlier. Clay knew of course that there'd been survivors from the stagecoach. The fancy one that afterwards his brother and he had tried to rob. And little they had gotten from it. Ike had ended up dead.

Clay didn't know what had happened to those survivors. For all he knew they could've left town for ever. He was too deep in grief for his brother to give a thought about what other folks might be doing.

The two had been brought up rough. They'd been thieves ever since they could walk, but neither of them had ever killed anybody, or even hurt anybody very bad. They had been part of the town for as long as Clay could remember.

There were mourners, with Clay, at Ike's funeral. Drinking partners mainly, plus a couple of local whores that the two had shared. But there were more folks to gawp at the sight of the notorious mad-dog killer, Brazos Tom, being put under the sod, including newspaper hacks and a feller with a new-fangled camera on kind of stilts. None of that sat well with Clay at all. I'll get back at them somehow, he thought.

Hell, he had to do something to bring him out of the grinding grief for his brother.

Clay went back to the saloon with the rest. With the topers the saloon always came after the wailing. One of the young whores tried taking Clay in hand, but he wasn't interested. Finally he sat in a corner, brooding over his booze, and folks left him alone.

He slipped away without anybody hardly noticing. He slept in the rickety cabin that Ike and he had shared for so many years, but as the night advanced he rose and crept out under the pale stars, glad that there was no moon. He'd make a kind of moon for them though, he'd do that all right.

At approximately the same time young Stefan was sitting on the edge of his cot in Doc Jock's place holding in his hand the gold half-hunter Pete Torlando had given him so that he could watch the time while he waited with the stolen cattle in the draw with the pool. And then there had been the wildcat . . . God, that seemed ages ago. But holding the watch now, the watch that his friend and chief had entrusted

116

to him, seemed to clinch things at last in Stefan's mind and he began to put his boots on.

At that time Brother Clay was silently prowling around the long coach that he'd visited before, but at that time of course, poor Ike had been with him.

In his hand Clay had a box of long-stemmed lucifers, the kind that sputtered and spat, igniting rapidly with a broad, bright flame.

It was easy to get inside the coach. Ike and he had done it before: practised burglars, they'd got into places that had been a helluva lot harder to breech than this one was . . .

Stefan knew how Brazos Tom had earlier got out of the surgery, only to meet his come-uppance not long after that. Stefan had hated Brazos Tom. It was ironical that the memory of that man and his short-lived escape should be of some help to Stefan now.

He discovered that the kitchen door was locked and bolted but the key was still in the lock. It was easy to get out into the night under the pale stars, a darkish night and he having to pick his way carefully with the walking stick.

He was unsure of exactly where the jailhouse lay. He didn't know what he could do when he got there. He felt that, anyway, he ought to try and talk to his friend and chief, Pete Torlando.

He ought to have a weapon — maybe he could do more then. He knew that his mind wasn't working as good as it should do, but he plodded on.

He didn't know that he was going in approximately the same direction that Brazos Tom had before him and that, at the moment, he was going away from the jailhouse instead of towards it. Here now in the full dark, the backs of town looked all alike. He looked for a door that he figured he might easily open. He had to get a weapon of some sort. His stick, though a stout one, was hardly adequate.

He turned into the very alley that Brazos Tom had traversed.

He came in sight of the strange, long

stagecoach that he'd heard about. He thought he saw movement there and he stopped dead, leaning on his stick, his heart thumping as he strove to get his breath back. Suddenly he was yearning to be back in his cot. What in hell did he think he was doing anyway — and what danger was ahead?

He did not turn, though. It was as if he could not . . .

14

Denny Trape said, 'I've been thinking. Folks saw them two characters come in but didn't see 'em come out again. It's bound to get around that we locked 'em up. We've only got two cells. Folks are gonna wonder about Torlando and Pedlar.'

Ep Lamister said, 'I've been thinking too.' He grinned. 'And I'll tell you what I'm gonna do. I'm gonna let those two out an' I'm gonna post 'em. Then in the middle o' the night we'll bring Pedlar and Torlando in here. There ain't so many folks trying to get at them now.'

Denny laughed. 'No, you kinda wore 'em out.'

One of the prisoners was snoring like a buzz-saw out of control. Denny went and shut the middle door. Ep said, 'We'll take it easy till Tubs gets back.'

The time passed. Then Tubs,

returned, watched the prisoners being released and, with Denny, listened to the sheriff's ultimatum to the two drowsy-looking hardcases.

'You can't do that,' said the one who hadn't talked before, going suddenly all bright and bushy-tailed, his poker-face more mobile than the bigger man's moustached visage.

The sheriff said, 'I can do it all right. If I see you in my town again I'll be gunning for you.'

Vocally now, Denny and Tubs agreed with this, both of them good with guns.

'We want our weapons back,' the leaner hardcase said.

'I'm commandeering them,' said Ep. 'Don't take any chances, boys, I'm warning you. I'm posting you outa my town an' you know what that means. Go get your horses and move.'

It was as if, suddenly, the two hardcases saw a different man, Denny Trape thought. The chief was a complex character who could be almighty ruthless. Denny hoped Ep was doing the right thing. But suddenly, almost dumbly, the erstwhile talky hardcase spoke for the first time since they'd let him out of his cell, and said, 'Hell, let's go anyway.' He looked tired and disgusted.

Tubs, carrying a levelled shotgun, saw them out of town. Then he went back to the office, and Ep said, 'Let's do the rest of it then.' They moved out back to the men who had been watching out for Torlando and Pedlar in their incarceration. Now the two villains would be going for a short *pasear* before being locked up again.

★ ★ ★

From the alley young Stefan saw the strange, long coach burst into flames, and at first he thought his eyes were playing tricks, thought maybe he was suddenly delirious. In truth, he didn't feel good at all. Had he been doing a foolish thing? He couldn't see anything near the coach now but the flames were spreading and the livery stable behind it was in danger.

Doc Jock came up the alley behind him. He had heard noises, got up, found Stefan's empty cot, had spotted him turning off the backs of town.

Now there was more light than there should be. Red light!

'I was just trying to walk, doc,' said Stefan weakly.

Doc caught the boy in his arms. Over Stefan's shoulder, he saw the flames spreading, reaching.

★   ★   ★

The two hardcases finished up in the circle of rocks where the bunch were waiting for them and Maybella demanded, 'Where in hell have you been?'

'We've been in jail,' the bigger, older, talkier one said.

The other one jerked a thumb in his companion's direction, a gesture of almost-disgust it seemed. He talked now. 'Jobey overplayed his hand. The sheriff got nasty an' slapped us in the cells. Then he 'posted' us.'

'Ep Lamister posted you?' echoed Joey Danco, always at Maybella's side it seemed.

'Yeh.'

'That's no empty threat,' said Maybella.

Danco said, 'If you were in the cells, where were Torlando and the other feller? How many cells are there in that jailhouse anyway?'

The moustached, talky hardcase was the subdued one now. His partner was coming out as the thinking one. 'We cut back. Came in behind the jail. There's some scrub there, enough to hide men and horses. The law had Torlando and his pardner in a cellar or somep'n. They fetched 'em out an' put 'em in the cells.'

'Well, you did somep'n after all,' said Maybella.

'It was my idea,' said the smaller, intelligent feller, giving his companion a hard sidelong glance.

'You'll stay with us,' said Maybella, evidently the leader. 'We're goin' in come late dark.'

'We fooled the law. They wouldn't know about you folk. And it looks like a lot o' the crowd that gathered in town from someplace else are leaving again.'

'We've got to get Stefan outa there as well,' said Maybella.

They were fidgety, waiting. Too risky to light a fire. Pulling at their canteens, smoking as the night grew long. No moon. Stars high up there.

They moved. Owlhooters all. Guerrillas, good with all kinds of weapons. Used to fighting by day or night and in all kinds of conditions. Led by a handsome, hard-bitten woman who was as good as any of them, a ruthless sharpshooter. And, at her side as always, the quiet killer called Joey Danco.

They saw the fire in the town, the great red gout. Maybella said, 'There's luck. There's our chance. Skirt away

125

from it, though.' She led the way.

She was the leader. Nobody — not even Joey — had disputed that. Still, although the rest of the boys didn't know it, it was Joey who'd talked her into taking this trick after she'd sent Torlando and Pedlar on their way, looking for Stefan: she'd been quite straight about that. This woman had her soft spots — and her love of Stefan — 'her boy' — was the softest. Even Joey accepted that.

Anyway, Joey wanted the boodle that Torlando and the others had gotten during the stagecoach holdup, and Torlando was the only one who could tell them where that was. It could have even been stashed someplace between Canyon Pass and Rancho Juanita and there was a hell of a lot of miles between those two settlements.

Maybella's anxiety about Stefan had been growing. They didn't know whether the boy was alive or dead. How could she trust Torlando, Joey had asked? It had been easy for him to talk

Maybella into this move. Hell, she was no wilting chippie. She was a good horsewoman and a fine shot. She had ridden with outlaws before on the owlhoot trail.

The fire was spreading. Folks were running about carrying buckets of water. A hose was being fixed to a pump. A wagon with two horses carried a sloshing water tank.

There was turmoil, the red light grotesquely illuminating yammering faces. Everybody wanted to help, but everybody didn't know what to do. The saloons had long since turned out, but everybody wasn't completely sober. They shouted a lot and ran about giving the alarm and cannoning into each other and into folks carrying water. Nobody was in charge. The men with the water wagon were being helped and a hose was jetting water, though not completely in the right direction. The fire seemed to have a malignant life of its own and it was spreading fiery tentacles, reaching out it seemed in all directions.

The visiting bunch were not crazy enough to come in all together. They didn't join up again until they were around the backs of town, and there was nobody there yet, the fire hadn't spread that far, though it seemed to be threatening to do so.

The bunch were all together again when they ran into Doc and Stefan at the back end of the alley where the red glow had paved a way. The bunch almost ran the struggling pair down.

'It's the kid,' said Joey Danco.

Doc Jock, still holding Stefan, shouted, 'What do you want?'

They milled around him.

He shouted, 'I've got to get this boy back inside before he drops.'

Maybella leapt from her saddle. 'Lead the way, old man.' She turned her head, looked up at Joey. 'I'll catch up with you.'

'You can't. You'll . . . '

'Do as I say.' The woman's voice was like a whiplash. Her gun was suddenly out as if she meant to shoot somebody.

She holstered it. She was dressed like a man, including a cartridge belt across her ample bosom, a gun rig.

She helped Doc and Stefan to the surgery. Her piebald horse, a favourite she had used a lot, waited patiently outside.

Stefan had weakly spoken her name, that was all.

They got him into the room that he had so recently vacated, got him on the cot. Maybella said, 'Make him fit to ride, old man.'

'I can't do that.'

'You'll do your damndest!' She drew her gun again, menace in her attitude, in her throaty voice.

'I will do my best. I always do.' Doc bent over Stefan who was only half-conscious, didn't seem to be noticing anything any more.

'You're taking a chance,' Doc Jock went on.

'Do your best then. I'll take that chance. I'll risk it.' The woman's voice had softened, strangely. She put her gun away again.

'It's not your risk,' the doc said curtly, over his shoulder.

Stefan moaned as if he were trying to say something.

15

Tubs was now at the source of the fire, keeping an eye on things, helping as much as he could, giving out with the orders if he had to. Most folks had always listened to him, except those who disliked the law. Some of those, given half the chance, would go around pillaging, vandalizing, looting.

The stagecoach was a smouldering ruin. Nobody knew how the fire had started. Brother Clay watched from a distance, seated on an upturned cast-iron bucket. Folks ran backwards and forwards in front of him. He looked like a very tired but still interested onlooker. Folks hardly noticed him. If anybody did they probably figured that he was still grieving for his brother. That was a fact. He was thinking now how much Ike would have enjoyed this spectacle.

The livery stable had now only

flickering flames but a lot of black smoke and it was slowly falling in upon itself. Its encumbents, old hostler Ben and boy Dick had been gotten out. The boy had had his scalp cooked a little, his hair singed. Doc Jock didn't seem to be anywhere around. The sheriff and his deputy, Denny, had stayed on at the jailhouse.

Three neighbours, one of whom owned the eating place under which Torlando and Pedlar had been briefly incarcerated, were on guard out back of the jail, the cell block.

The man who had property to save had to leave as somebody yelled that the fire was spreading because the wind was suddenly getting up in the once-still night. The devils of the elements were playing up. Godamighty, the messenger said, exaggeratedly, the whole damn' town could burn.

The other two surrogate deputies, both of whom lived in town — one with a wife and kids — began to get jittery. The married one ran into the office.

'Ep, we've got to do somep'n . . . '

'All right, Abe. Go on.'

Ep added, 'Stay here, Denny. I'll go out back.' He followed Abe out.

The horsemen crouching in the brush not far from the back of the jail watched everything that was going on. Their mounts were out of sight behind them but within easy reach. The glow of the fires gave a fitful light, but it was still pretty dark out here with the stars high, no moon, the wind freshening but of no consequence to the watching outlaws.

They saw the man going back home, the sheriff talking to the other one.

'Take 'em,' said Joey Danco and rose, gun in hand.

He moved out of cover and, already spread out, the others followed him. Right away they started shooting.

Ep Lamister was partly sheltered by the man he was talking to. Although he hadn't known it till the trouble started, luck was with him — up to a point anyway.

The other man, virtually drilled in many places, collapsed against his friend the sheriff, was driven into him by the impact of the slugs. Ep was forced backwards and went to his knees, drawing his gun, levelling it, thumbing the hammer the fast way. A star-packer, he was also a hammer-slammer. Both attributes had served him well, were doing this again. He saw one man spin and fall and lie still, saw another drop to his knees, head hanging. In a short lull in the gunfire, the echoes rolling and fading, Ep heard the man screaming.

The others were taking what cover they could, and there wasn't much of that now. Two of them retreated to the brush. One threw himself flat on the ground. The man they aimed to kill was being protected by a dead friend. But now, with one hand, Ep began to drag the body back into the outer door of the jailhouse, while firing with his other hand until his gun was empty.

He had almost made it to the cover

when a blow as if from a red-hot branding iron smote him in the head and he felt himself falling — and then the blackness closed over him.

The outlaws, with Joey Danco, unhurt, leading them, clambered over the two bodies.

They burst into the cell-block and came under the startled gaze of the prisoners they had come to rescue. Danco shouted, 'Stand back.'

Torlando and Pedlar retreated to the back walls.

Working like part of the team to which they belonged, two of the men, guns levelled, went through the other door which led into the office.

Danco blew the locks of the cell-doors off with well-placed pistol shots. The door swung open and the two prisoners came out amid the swirling, dissipating black smoke.

At the middle door, Denny Trape put a bullet into the belly of one of the two outlaws who had almost cannoned into him. The second man, gun-barrel elevated, fired past his agonizingly twisted, wounded friend and, hit by a bullet that ploughed through his cheekbone and upwards, Deputy Denny collapsed to the boards, rolled over, became still.

The wounded outlaw, groaning with the agony from his perforated gut, was dragged out. Another wounded man was hauled on to a horse. The two still forms in the outer doorway were dragged aside. The bunch worked fast. They left one of their own dead outside the jail. They hadn't missed a thing, had brought spare horses for Torlando and Pedlar.

They went out of Canyon Pass in the opposite direction to the way they'd come in, avoiding the area where the fire was bad. A few bemused folk saw them go, didn't get in their way, didn't even shout after them. They were out in a quiet spot when Danco gave orders to rein in. He went back alone.

He saw two riders approaching him. Erect in the saddle, one of them waved.

He could not mistake Maybella for anybody else, didn't even wave back, waited till they came up to him, the smaller figure tied in the saddle, slumping, but easily recognizable as young Stefan.

Maybella said, 'The doc gave him a draught of something to ease him. He's in a bad way still so we'll have to go easy.'

'Not too easy,' said Danco. 'What about the doc?'

'I let him go. I guess he'll go to the sheriff.'

'The sheriff ain't gonna help much. Let's move.' Danco wheeled his horse about.

★　★　★

There was the crash of timbers and the roar of flames, but some folks had heard the shooting. What could they do about it: it wasn't near them? Somebody said the gunshop had caught fire. Folks were saving themselves and their property. If anybody was shooting at anybody else, nobody it seemed had seen them. Anyway, they were caring for themselves and their people. Shooting was the law's business.

The gunshop was run by Steve Smildey, Tub's son, and the boy's wife: they had no offspring yet. Deputy Tubs ran to them, was relieved to find that so far they had escaped the fire, were helping neighbours who'd caught the edge of it.

The fires, except for a few small blazes here and there, were dying out.

Nobody had been badly hurt — which was a mercy . . .

Deputy Tubs, in the thick of the action, with cracking timbers around him, hadn't heard any shooting. There hadn't been any guns going off at the shop, which would be all right. Tubs ran from there to the jailhouse. He didn't know that Doc Jock had beaten him to that place.

The doc saw the body on the ground by the back door, another body near,

Ep Lamister leaning over it, his face streaming with blood.

'Leave him,' snarled Ep, getting on one knee beside the second blood-stained form. 'This is neighbour Caleb an' he got what was meant for me.' His voice broke but, when Doc moved to help him, broke out again more fully, 'All I've got is a damn crease. Denny is back there in the office.'

Doc went past him, past the body of volunteer Deputy Caleb, through the door, the cell-block, noting the open barred doors, the communicating one ajar also. Denny lay just beyond that, in the glare of the hanging lamp . . .

Doc, half-down, straightened, whirled about as the street door was hammered.

'Who's there?'

'It's me — Tubs.'

Doc unlocked the door, let the deputy in. Tubs saw the body, the blood. Jock said, 'You can't do anything for Denny. Come and help me with Ep.'

Tubs took the large red-and-white-checked handkerchief out of his pocket and placed it gently over the young deputy's ruined face, then he followed his old friend, Doc Jock, out to the sheriff who was now staggering through the cell-block towards them.

16

The bunch had left one of their own, dead, back in Canyon Pass. They were lugging two wounded back with them, one with a slug in the belly, the second one with a slug in the hip. There was some consolation that they had left dead law behind.

They had accomplished what they had set out to do, so maybe they were riding high. Except for the two wounded boys, of course, who shouldn't have been in the saddle at all and filled the night with their lamentations.

The two rescued men were vocal also. At first they were full of thanks to their deliverers. They had a horse apiece, and good ones. They asked for guns, but Maybella wouldn't allow them any weapons at all.

They asked, Why not? There was no

plain answer. Maybella was adamant. Her sidekick Joey Danco told them to quit their belly-aching or maybe they'd be left behind. Pete Torlando said that'd be all right by him: they'd go in a different direction. But Maybella wouldn't even let them do that. She said Joey had only been joshing, and Joey himself laughed immoderately at the quip.

Maybella had been soft, but now she was hard again — except when her glance strayed towards Stefan. They'd got him out too, but he was in no better shape than the two wounded boys, though he wasn't making as much noise as they were.

He had been wrapped in a thick, voluminous saddle-blanket and tied to a saddle. They had slipped up somewhat, had brought horses for Torlando and Pedlar but not for Stefan. Still, they hadn't known whether he'd survived or not. Even so, Maybella had been mighty peeved at the oversight. A horse had had to be stolen complete with saddle and that small task had been accomplished.

Still and all, they figured they hadn't done too badly. The boys figured that their lady boss shouldn't be complaining all the time like she had a sore ass or something. Then when, in a small draw, Maybella drew them to a halt, they jibed. She told them to shut up.

The man with the belly wound had shut up, and it was discovered that he was dead.

While Maybella tried to make Stefan more comfortable, the others quickly made a long shallow hole, put the dead outlaw's body in there and covered it with rocks and soil.

Stefan was lapsing in and out of consciousness and Maybella couldn't do much for him. She and the others had taken their attention off Torlando and Pedlar for a while, however, and the latter took a foolish chance. He grabbed a gun out of a bending man's holster.

What he meant to do with it wasn't

clear. He didn't live to explain. Joey Danco, who had a draw like a snake's tongue, shot him in the middle of the forehead.

Pedlar's partner, Pete Torlando backed off, said; 'What did you do that for?' which sounded pretty stupid coming from him.

'Don't you try anything like that,' Danco said. 'I don't want to have to shoot you as well.'

'What's the game?'

'Get back on your horse, Pete,' said Maybella. 'That shot might've been heard. We've got to get away from here.'

'What about him?' Danco indicated the body lying on its back, staring up at the pale stars.

'Sling it over his horse.'

Everybody began to move quickly again.

* * *

That was the truth, Clay Teller told himself, he hadn't meant to set the town on fire — just their damn' fancy coach. Just to sort of get back at them. Just a gesture.

He didn't know whether anybody had actually seen him hanging around by the coach before the alarm was given. Even a drunk, for instance, who might bring him to mind later when memory returned after the effects of the booze had been slept off.

Clay himself had had mornings like that. He'd also had mornings when, after a hard session with the firewater, he couldn't bring back a thing except maybe a lot of puke.

Oh, to hell with it, he thought. He was sitting up in bed and the early morning sun was slipping through the window. There was no sound from outside. In the cot opposite no brother Ike was mumbling to himself as he often did, awakening Clay. Ike wasn't there. He would never wake Clay up again.

Ike was dead, his body in the undertaker's parlour. Clay wouldn't even see his brother buried. Of a sudden he had made his mind up completely. He had to get out of this town. Ike would understand! He got up and dressed, washed himself in cold water at the small cast-iron pump. Soon he was guiding his horse along the backs and, finally, out on to the trail. He didn't see a soul. Some of the town hadn't been touched by the fire. Serve 'em right anyway, Clay tried to tell himself, but he couldn't be too sure about that.

He kept looking back as if he figured somebody was following him. But nobody was.

Once he jerked the horse's head around, making the beast blink. It was as if the town was trying to pull him back. He had known that town much, much more than he had any other. But . . .

'Go on, yuh,' he said, and the horse was going in a straight line again, hooves rising up and down rhythmically. And the trail rolled ahead of them, empty under the sun.

After Ep Lamister's wife died in childbirth, Ep rented his house out to a couple with two kids. He learned that the house had caught fire but wasn't destroyed. The man had sustained a few burns, would be all right; he had saved his wife and kids and they were fine.

Doc Jock admitted that Ep's head wound was not as bad a 'crease' as the elderly medico had at first thought. He didn't think the sheriff was prime enough to go galloping away, but he didn't tell Ep that, knowing that the man aimed to go trailing as soon as possible, as would be expected of him.

Ep now lived in the annexe beside the jailhouse. He didn't stay long. And already Tubs Smildey was rounding up a willing posse.

The sheriff was driving himself, and that was a fact. Fury and impatience were eating at him.

If he hadn't moved Torlando and Pedlar into the cell-block maybe Denny

147

would still be alive, as well as the luckless neighbour, Caleb, who had been shot outside . . .

But if they had learned about the cellar where the two prisoners had first been kept — Lordy, how'd they found out about *anything* — and attacked that, the jail-breakers might have slaughtered all three neighbours who were not regular deputies but just law-abiding and willing citizens, great friends of Ep's, as Denny had been, he almost a son to his widowed chief . . .

Sheriff Ep Lamister, a disciplined and forthright man, shut these unanswerable questions out of his mind, bottled up his grief and his pointless fury. He barked his orders and led his men out of town, all of them pledged — he knew this! — not to return until their bloody task was done.

* * *

The second wounded hardcase fell out of the saddle and lay on the

148

ground, moaning.

Pete Torlando said, 'You ought to shoot him I guess.'

Joey Danco snarled, 'Shut up, yuh.'

He thought, but maybe the feller has a point. The wounded man had only been shot in the hip, was whining too much.

There were rocks ahead, shelter of a sort. 'Let's get him in there,' Maybella said.

He screamed as they loaded him back on the saddle like a sack of logs. Maybella was peeved about that, snapped, 'Stow your noise!'

The man was silent. In the rocks they off-loaded him again and the woman took a look, rearranged his bandages, which had been done in a hurry earlier. Then, from her saddle-bag, Maybella raked out a bottle of whisky, and told the man to take a good swig of it.

Soon he was half-conscious, mumbling to himself. Now, however, the lady chieftain was more involved with young Stefan who said, 'I'll be all right,' but didn't look too good at all.

There was a man on watch outside the rock outcrop, a rifle sloped in one hand, his other paw shading his eyes from the sun which was at its zenith and like a red-hot ball.

The watcher saw the oncoming horse and rider like a mirage out of the heat haze, a shimmering figure that became slowly larger but then seemed to hesitate.

The rifleman did not shout but, almost unconsciously, he raised his weapon, though not completely yet to his shoulder. He didn't know who this galoot was.

The horseman — it was Clay Teller — had seen the man in the front of the jumbled rocks, had seen the sun glinting on the barrel of the rifle.

Clay was no quickshooter, but he carried the inevitable six-gun. He had only just realized that he had left his own rifle back at the house he had shared with his brother Ike: a hovel, anybody was welcome to it now.

Ike had always insisted that weapons should be cleaned and primed.

It hurt Clay to keep thinking of Ike, to be reminded of him in so many ways. And only a little while ago it had seemed that that town back there was pulling at him, that he shouldn't have left it.

It was long behind . . .

He pulled his gun, raised it, levelled it, fired.

The slug did not hit its target properly — Clay had been too hasty anyway. The speeding slug whacked the barrel of the rifle and knocked it from the lookout man's hand.

The hardcase dropped on one knee, sucking his stinging fingers. Hell, his hand could've been busted altogether! With his other paw, he reached for the rifle. His fingers were still not right, a numbness coming on them. He couldn't level the rifle and shoot again right away.

He was able to lift the hand, though, and shade his eyes with it, and he saw that the strange horseman had turned his mount about and was beating a hasty retreat. Horse and rider disappeared in the heat haze.

Joey Danco ran out of the rocks. 'What in hell . . . ?'

'A rider. He took a shot at me.'

'And that shot might've been heard. Get back in here.'

Maybella came in sight, silhouetted on the rocks like a spectre of condemnation. She must have heard the brief exchange between her two sidekicks. Everybody had heard the shot.

Behind the tall, handsome woman there was a small buzz of voices.

'Move,' Maybella screamed. 'Move!'

17

The law party were too far away to have heard the shot, but Clay Teller, coming at them suddenly from out of the sun like an apparition, almost got perforated himself.

His horse came to a halt in a flurry of dust. 'I was out ridin',' Clay said loudly, then he began to cough.

Sheriff Lamister said, 'You've come a long way.'

'I was just about to turn back,' Clay lied, 'then I saw a feller with a rifle an' he took a shot at me.'

He wondered whether, if the shot had been heard by the posse, anybody had been able to identify the sound as a hand-gun explosion rather than one made by a rifle.

He needn't have worried. He went on, 'I think there was a bunch in some rocks.'

The sheriff shouted, 'Let's move.' Clay was about to be swept out of the way. His horse skittered, pranced. The dust rose again. Clay shouted hoarsely, 'I'm comin' with you.'

Ep Lamister didn't seem to object, hadn't got time to say anything. Clay joined in with the rest, didn't know why he'd done this. He didn't have to go back to town, could have veered off in another direction from the posse after he'd left them. And away from the bunch which he figured were straight ahead, though probably too far to be caught up with, unless they lay in wait.

Clay decided he wasn't fazed either way. Maybe he'd get a shot at that bastard who'd tried to pop him.

They saw the coyote first, running out of a draw which proved to be shallow. And then they saw the vultures high in the sky. They reined in at the shallow dip, the small disturbed bundle of small rocks.

Ep said, 'That coyote must've nosed and pawed at this. Get the rest off.'

Complaining, the vultures had moved higher in the sky, hovering.

'It's a body.' It was recognizable too.

'It's one o' those characters I posted,' said Ep. 'And he's been shot. Cover 'im up again.'

It was done. Better than before maybe. Hurried though. Ep was anxious to move on.

'I came by here,' said Clay. 'I didn't see anything then. That other place is straight on.'

'At least we're on the right line then,' said Ep sardonically.

'One posted an' one to go,' quipped Tubs Smildey.

'And more than that,' said Ep, all grimness again.

★   ★   ★

Maybella and her bunch halted again a few miles on the North American side of the Rio Grande — for various reasons. The boy with a bullet in his hip was suffering. Nobody had had time to

155

take the offending slug out. The bunch wanted a wagon, not for the boy with the bullet in his hip but for Stefan who seemed to be even worse off than the boy with a bullet in his hip. Maybella was mighty worried about Stefan.

The place on the river approach was run by a dark-skinned runty individual called Dink. He was wanted by the *rurales* over the border and had fled. They were glad to get rid of him: as far as they were concerned the gringos could have him, and good riddance. Now he sold anything useful to anybody who passed by, and Maybella had used him before.

Besides — he could keep his mouth shut. He knew where his bread was well-buttered, and that was on this side of the big river. If he ventured over those placid waters he'd likely get his ass shot off.

The boy with the bullet in his hip didn't want to stay with Dink, though Dink, among other things, claimed to have medical knowledge. At least he'd get that slug out and then the boy could rest up. He'd hide him too, if anybody came a-looking.

Maybella paid Dink well. Pete Torlando said, 'It would've been cheaper to shoot the little cuss.'

Joey Danco, who stood behind Torlando at that time, drew a swift gun, pressed the cold barrel to the back of Torlando's neck and said, 'If I shoot you instead Dink can bury you for us.'

Dink, who knew Torlando and his reputation, licked suddenly dry lips, wondering what was going on. But Torlando said, 'You won't do that, Joey.' And Joey didn't.

The trail led to a usually shallow part of the big river, and it was even shallower right now after the broiling heat that had been around during the last few days.

The horsemen crossed without mishap. The wagon-wheels didn't sink too deeply and Stefan, wrapped like a mummy in blankets, didn't make a sound.

Maybella said, 'We'll go right home,' which was what they had been expecting to do all along.

Joey had tentatively suggested that they bide in the stockade at Dink's place and wait to see if anybody was following and, if a bunch was, bushwhack them. Torlando had said that, if such was the case, they ought to give him a gun. That had brought more ribald complaints from Joey who seemed to be delighted at having the famous leader road-agent at his mercy.

Joey had even suggested that they should leave Stefan with Dink for that man's care, and Maybella had said she didn't want the boy to fall into 'that law's' hands again. And Joey had sniggered as he often did but had said nothing more after that.

So their next stop would be Rancho Juanita and, once there, they could chase off a damned army, Maybella had said. Joey had had to agree with that, not letting his evil mouth run away with him any more.

While they were at Dink's place night had fallen. The crossing of the river had been a cooling thing after the heat of the day but, as they moved further into Mexico, the skies became darker than they had been and the air was like a furnace breath as if presaging a storm.

Their numbers were depleted: they had left something else back at Dink's place apart from the boy with a bullet in his hip . . .

* * *

Ep Lamister said, 'We're getting near to Dink's place.'

Tubs Smildey said, 'I remember that.'

'He's got a sort of stockade where he used to keep his horses, maybe still does. We'll make a half-circle an' come in back of it.'

'Yeh, it could be a prime place for an ambush.'

'I don't think somehow that that bunch will aim to do that. I think they'll want to get over the river as soon as

159

they can and make for Rancho Juanita.'
Ep was remembering that last time he'd
ridden this way Denny had been with
him. Such a short time ago, but such a
sorrowful time in between.

The night was dark and humid. Tubs
had said he thought a storm was brewing.

Conditions had been good to them
so far, however. Cutting in after their
detour, they saw spare lights in back of
Dink's place and Ep called a halt.

One of them said, 'I heard somep'n.'

Somebody else said, 'Sounds like
somebody digging.'

It was late. And a ghostly sound.

Ep and Tubs went forward on foot.

Stunted Dink was digging a grave. A
body lay beside it. He straightened to
face the glint of two levelled guns.

'Who's that?'

'It's Ep Lamister, Dink,' whispered
the burly sheriff.

'And Tubs Smildey,' said his companion. 'What you doin', boy?' The plump
deputy went forward, struck a lucifer,
shielding the flame with his cupped

hand as he held it over the face of the corpse. Ep still kept the digger covered, said 'Lower the shovel gently, bucko.' And Dink did as he was told.

'It's Dick Pedlar,' said Tubs. 'He's bin shot in the head.'

'Do tell! So that bunch did come this way like we figured. They shore left a signal here, could've been wavin' a flag.'

'I guess they didn't figure we'd get here so soon. They ain't still here, are they, Dink?'

'No.'

Seemed like the question hadn't needed an answer anyway. The silence was as deep as the grave itself until the sheriff called the rest of his men forward. Then all the men dismounted and watched Dink finish his task. And then Dink was ushered into the kitchen of his house and there was nobody else waiting there.

'I was told that Joey Danco shot Pedlar. I don't know what it was all about. I've done business with May-bella before. They had a sick boy with 'em, as well as the dead 'un which needed burying. Seemed Maybella had figured to take him home to friends of his in Rancho Juanita. But she changed her mind.'

'Mebbe he was turning ripe,' said one of the visitors. But nobody laughed.

'I let Maybella have a buckboard so they could transport the sick boy. They left another one behind . . . ' Dink paused. Maybe for dramatic effect. Despite his looks — the low brow and shaggily-hidden eyes — he was an accomplished confidence-man.

The sudden appearance of the law party had, however, fazed him somewhat. The astute Ep knew that. He'd never heard Dink talk so much. In the old days the man had been as close-mouthed as a gopher with jaw-ache. Ep couldn't help reflect that, if Maybella knew Dink was gabbing as much as this — particularly to the law — she'd like to have his head blown off.

'A feller with a bullet wound. I took the slug out. He's upstairs.' Dink even led the way, the sheriff and his deputy at his heels.

Dink knew how Ep could be. The man had put on weight and maybe he wasn't as fast as he used to be. But this wasn't Mexico where Dink could maybe hide, even though the *rurales* there wanted his head. This was North America borderlands and Ep was well-known, even well-liked; feared and respected too. Oh, yes, Ep could make things hot for Dink all right.

The wounded boy woke from sleep as the three men entered his room. Ep reflected sardonically that in the old days Dink had kept a couple of fancy whores up here. This blinking boy was no substitute.

'We're the law from Canyon Pass and if you don't tell us all we want to know, boy, we're gonna hang you.' The big man's voice was cold as ice, and his plump older companion grinned like an evil Cheshire cat and said, 'Durn tootin'.'

Oh, he told them all he knew, that boy, but not much they didn't know already — except Joey Danco and Pete Torlando being at loggerheads and Maybella not allowing Torlando to tote a weapon. That knowledge puzzled Ep a mite at first; but then not quite so much. Maybella had to be the kingpin, the queen bee. Even Joey sank small to her, as it suited him.

But there was a lot of boodle at stake!

Dink had one of his minions bring coffee and oatcakes which the posse members drained and wolfed. They replenished their canteens. Then they were on their way again, but not before their leader had a few more pregnant words to say to Dink.

'You stay quiet an' easy and don't talk to anybody or I'll come back an' grab your ass and tote you back over the Rio an' feed you to the *rurales*.'

Dink gave a guttural laugh with no humour in it at all, asked, 'What do I do with the wounded boy?'

'Keep him here. We'll pick him up on

the way back, I guess.' Having said that, Ep reflected, will we be back and, if so, how many of us will be able to call here again? Maybe the wounded boy, who didn't seem too bad now, would have the best of it after all. One thing you had to say for ugly Dink, he'd always kept a cosy billet. He'd double-cross his own mother, if he'd ever had one: a rattlesnake maybe. And if somehow he'd got to hear about the stolen bullion he'd want to cut himself a piece or two.

But, riding his men out now, Ep Lamister, gunfighter avenger, didn't have any more time to waste in his head figuring whether ugly Dink would play his cards on top of the deck or not . . .

Ep didn't realize, until he was told, that Clay Teller was missing. He said, 'I was kinda wonderin' about him . . . '

Tubs Smildey said, 'Me too . . . '

Ep said, 'Waal, there's nothin' we can do about that now.' And that was a fact! They both figured that maybe they'd never see young Clay ever again.

18

Pete Torlando said, 'All right then, a three-way split.' He owed Maybella *dinero*. But he hadn't expected there would have to be so much. He was at her mercy now, however, and with her paramour Joey who'd plumb prefer a two-way split if he could have his way. Unarmed as he'd been all along on the trail, Maybella was his only chance of survival, and his pickings would still be mighty rich anyhow.

He was the outsider in Maybella's bailiwick. He could be tortured. He could be killed. But, in a sense, he still held the shaky whiphand: *only he knew where the boodle was stashed*.

Accompanied by the woman and her fancy man he led the way out of Rancho Juanita and they made sure they weren't followed.

They hit the rocky territory a few

miles out of town. The morning sun was rising but partly obscured by drifting mists. The air was as hot as the bowels of hell.

Suddenly the light was gone and the day exploded in thunder and the rain came down in sheets.

They spurred their horses to nearby rocks and tried to shelter as best they could.

'How much further?' Maybella shouted.

'Not far,' Torlando shouted back. The rain was like liquid thunder-claps.

Joey didn't say anything. The way he was, he'd kept a gun on Torlando. Now he pouched it to keep it from the rain. Head down, cold water running down his neck, Pete Torlando smiled mirthlessly to himself and reflected, if I could get that weapon I'd shoot these two dead and let them lie: they've surely asked for it!

And maybe that was what they had planned for him once they had the loot. Joey would like that! Torlando and

Maybella had been friends and lovers before the former went on the owlhoot and Joey came along. But money — that much money! — could be a great goad.

They had half-expected this storm while they were riding last night after they had crossed the big river at the shallow point with the wagon-wheels barely covered and young Stefan as comfortable and dry as a snail in a shell in a warm thicket.

They had brought their slickers with them this morning, but the deluge had come so suddenly, they hadn't had time to put them on. Torlando struggled into his, knowing that Joey was watching him like a hawk, the lean, saturnine young man's hand back on the butt of his gun.

Maybella got into her garment too, but both she and Torlando were only covering their unpleasant wetness. Joey, hunkered against a rock, stayed as he was, as if impervious to the deluge that soaked him to the skin.

Maybe we'll all perish, Torlando thought, washed away in dirty flood water; and the boodle would stay in the ground, dry and hidden, until eternity. The thought amused him but he did not laugh.

★ ★ ★

Tubs said, 'You've taken that thing off your haid that Doc Jock put there.'

Ep said, 'It irritates me.'

'Hell's bells, you should've had it bandaged properly.'

'Then I wouldn't have been able to get my hat on, would I? And in this heat I'd be fryin' now, and useless.'

'You shouldn't even be riding. The doc said . . .'

'The doc ain't allus right.' In truth, though, Ep had a splitting headache. But he blamed this on the heat. Tubs, exasperated, quit talking.

They had had a short rest by night after leaving Dink's place. But Ep wanted to press on and nobody had argued about that, not even Tubs.

It was still early morning, the sun just coming up, when the rain began. The boys hit a stroke of luck, however, and sheltered in a falling-down barn. Adjacent to it was a patch of black ground as if a fire had razed whatever else had stood there.

The boys and their horses all managed to get into cover, mostly avoiding the drips and drops that fell from the shattered timbers. This was a hell of a storm. The noise of it made conversation difficult. The boys smoked and swore.

The rain was still coming fast, though it seemed to be abating a mite. Ep yelled, 'Have you all got slickers?'

Yes, fearing that the rain would come eventually after the breathtaking heat, everybody had brought a slicker, could be well covered.

'We'll go on to Rancho Juanita,' Ep went on. 'We won't be noticed so much in this downpour.'

He added, with forced jocularity,

'Keep your powder dry.'

Nobody actually laughed.

Tubs Smildey wasn't sure whether riding into Rancho Juanita in daylight was a good idea, rain or not and, as they rode on, he reflected on this. Maybella and Danco had their own bunch, but that was depleted; the bunch riding with Tubs and Ep now could match them. The rest of the populace of that outlaw town would be inclined to keep their noses out of things. They'd probably have nefarious schemes of their own going along. It was pretty certain that nobody else would know about the boodle that might be the centre of everything that had gone down lately, including the jailbreak.

As for the folks who'd pulled off the bullion robbery, the hold-up of the show-off stagecoach — only one of them was left. Pete Torlando. His last partner Dick Pedlar had been killed by Joey Danco, or so runty Dink had reported. He'd buried the body and, as far as the law could determine, right now Dink had no axe to grind.

Tubs reflected that if this bunch wanted to get into their destination by night they'd have to wait a full day, hanging low, powerless. Things hadn't worked out quite as they might have done. Tubs knew that Ep wouldn't wait. Actually Tubs had to admit that he didn't much feel like waiting himself, and he figured that none of the rest of the boys would want that either.

Still and all, Tubs couldn't stop worrying about Ep. He noticed that the big man squinted against the rain in a strange way, kept raising his head as if to make sure he wasn't going to ride his horse into some obstacle. I reckon he's got a blinding headache and won't admit it, Tubs thought. He hoped that Ep could see all right, wearing spectacles as he did for close work, just as Tubs himself did.

Ep was mighty good with a handgun. So was Tubs, but he knew he wasn't nearly as fast and accurate as Ep could be. They'd need every advantage, this bunch; and, although Tubs had half-way reassured himself, he had to admit also that they didn't know what the hell they were going into and — a gruesome thought — some of them mightn't ever see home again.

★   ★   ★

The rain had lost some of its early fury and the sun was out. Maybella and Danco rode abreast with Torlando a little way ahead of them. Danco had put a duster over top of his other wet garments, saying he aimed to keep his shooter dry. Maybella and Torlando both wore slickers which they had donned earlier. There was desolation all around them, but they were now approaching rockier terrain and Torlando had said they hadn't much further to go.

He skirted an outcrop of rocks and the other two watched him carefully, Danco pushing his horse closer, one hand on his reins, the other hidden under his coat, the fist obviously gripping the butt of his revolver.

Torlando reined in suddenly and, without a word, slid down from his saddle.

'Do you want this?' Danco halted too, hugged his horse's flanks with his knees, his right hand still on his gun-butt, the left one holding forth the sharp-pointed digging shovel that he had been carrying on his saddle. He hadn't trusted Torlando with such a potential weapon.

'I'll take it,' said Torlando, moving forward.

'Stop!' snapped Danco. As if by swift sleight of hand, his gun appeared. Torlando pulled up dead before the levelled steel barrel winking wickedly in the pale sun.

Danco covered most of the gun with the end of his long duster. He let the digging implement fall from his other hand. 'Pick it up,' he snarled.

Torlando shrugged, unspeaking. He

bent and picked up the shovel.

Maybella said, 'Get to it, Pete.'

Torlando, straightened, spoke up. 'You don't have to treat me bad, either of you. I've been straight with you all along. I've promised you a third each and I'll stick by that. Hell, I'll be getting more even so than I would have gotten in the first place, ain't I? We said that.' He was turning away, the digger swinging in his hand. 'I don't understand you, don't understand you at all.' The words floated back over his shoulder.

Momentarily bereft of words, the other man and the woman slid down from their horses and followed Torlando who was strolling well ahead of them now. He stopped suddenly and they stopped too, Danco still with his gun pulled, sheltered by his coat, only a glimpse of the gleaming barrel.

The rain came down steadily and against it the sun was a poor thing.

The digging implement sang as it hit the ground — and then Torlando was bending, digging.

'You can spell me, Joey,' he shouted, still with a good breath in him.

'Don't count on that, bucko,' Joey shouted back.

Maybella didn't say anything. Her fine dark eyes shone, their gaze on the working man who said nothing more, worked powerfully, methodically. He soon had a pile of soil, shale and small loose rocks beside him.

He paused to wipe his brow with the back of his hand, sweat mingling with the rain, getting in his eyes.

'Take a turn, Joey.'

'Like hell!'

But then Torlando seemed to hit something. He paused again, and the other two watched him avidly.

He let the shovel fall, bent his back and used both his hands like claws, hidden now from the other man, and the speechless bright-eyed woman.

He took a well-wrapped sack from the hole and placed it at the side. Nothing would have penetrated that hole. The dust that drifted from the sack was dry until the rain hit it.

Torlando took up the shovel again, dug a little more, then put the implement to one side for a second time. He bent, his hands dipping.

He seemed to be struggling, as if something was stuck down there.

He came up suddenly, swinging to one side, steel flashing in his hand. Danco triggered his gun. The bullet went past Torlando's head and whined away into nothingness. Already the knife was on its way in the other direction, thrown with all the power of the lean man's muscular torso behind it.

The razor-sharp, gleaming, pointed steel blade embedded itself deeply beneath Danco's breastbone. The man went over backwards as if he'd been kicked by a high-stepping workhorse suddenly gone loco with the heat and the rain.

Danco's heels kicked up. The back of his head hit the ground, hard. His legs straightened out then. Full length. He became still and it was as if he was already laid out for burying.

His gun, spinning upwards from his hand, had fallen on the edge of the hole that Torlando had worked on.

He picked up the weapon.

Maybella was standing with her arms out at her sides, the fingers of her hands spread, empty.

Torlando said, 'Take that gun outa your waist slowly, honey, and drop it on the ground.'

She did this. The weapon was smaller than the average Colt and had a yellow bone butt chased in silver. A wicked pistol, and Torlando knew that the woman was good with it. He said, 'Now that little reticule with the derringer in it. Drop that too. Easy. *Easee-ee.*'

It was a little black silk bag, little more than pouch. It made a metallic sound as it hit the hard sod which not even the driving rain had penetrated yet.

'I wasn't goin' to try anything,' said

Maybella, her contralto voice sounding almost gentle.

Torlando said, 'He meant to kill me. You know that.'

'He was unpredictable and kind of stupid. He didn't know you as well as I do. I figured you'd pull something.'

'I was gonna put a gun down there. Then I thought maybe the dust 'ud get in it or somep'n — and I couldn't wrap it. Maybe I'd need it fast. If I needed it at all. A knife was best.'

'Yeh,' said the woman, looking at the body. 'He had to try didn't he? Pity. I liked him.'

'You liked me once.'

'I still do, always will.'

A dialogue in the rain. 'So you say.' The man talking again. As if he didn't know what he aimed to do when he stopped. A form of harsh laughter expelled from his lips as, still with his eyes on the woman, he picked up the lethal pistol and the reticule containing Maybella's almost equally lethal double-shot derringer.

He backed off a little, picked up one of the two sacks containing bullion and dropped the two guns into that. He put his own Colt back in its holster.

Upright, thumbs tucked in his belt, he looked straight at the woman. Then he backed to his horse and fastened the two bags to the saddle, but he was still looking at her all the time — and he finally said, 'I'm ridin' further into Mexico. You comin'?'

She said, 'I've got to go back to young Stefan. He ain't out of the woods yet.' Her voice became suddenly vehement. 'And you owe him, don't you?'

The man seemed to reflect on this, momentarily. Then he said, 'Guess I do. I'll come with you. We'll get a buckboard, take him out. But we've got to be fast. Mount up!'

19

In a bid to take a shorter cut to Rancho Juanita, Ep Lamister led his men across rocky land, a sort of miniature bad-lands.

A horse stumbled, lost a shoe, almost tossed its rider from the saddle. The man dismounted, said, 'I'll have to lead him.'

'You do that, Perce.' Then, after pausing a mite, Ep went on. 'As I remember, there used to be a small-holding past this patch. I guess we can get you another mount there.' He proved to be right. They spotted a cluster of worn-down buildings which turned out to contain a somewhat worn-down farmer with a wife and two kids.

Somebody said they could've gotten spare cayuses from Dink's place. But Ep said that Dink only had plugs nowadays. Still, would this place have any better? In the back of his mind was another thought that he couldn't shake. If they hadn't taken this trail Perce's horse wouldn't have suffered. And they sure as hell hadn't saved any time at all.

The dirt farmer had two working plugs but also a dun mare, not a youngster but still a sturdy riding beast. He was willing to sell her. Ep gave him the *dinero* he asked for.

Perce loaded his gear on to the mare which the farmer said was called Dusey. He said he'd look after Perce's horse. The latter nuzzled the man as if taking a fancy to him.

The boys came away from the pump where they had been refreshing themselves and their mounts. And they went on their way.

'If that man fixes him good I'll go later an' buy ol' Pard back,' Perce said.

'Maybe you won't want to,' said Tubs Smildey, watching the dun mare called Dusey stepping lively.

Despite their urgency to get going, Maybella held Torlando up, insisting that they bury Joey Danco. She wielded the shovel and the man did the best he could with his feet. Joey was buried in the hole which had contained the boodle he had coveted so much. Torlando didn't say any words of any kind, but Maybella was heard to murmur 'So long, Joey' (whatever that meant) before they finally left the area and made speed for Rancho Juanita.

The rain was abating at last, but their horses' hooves made sloshing sounds as they moved, not after all going so fast, the spare horse trotting cheerfully behind the rest. The little settlement was quiet and they went straight to Maybella's place to be greeted by Ginger Lil, Maybella's *segundo* and best sister-like friend, a big woman in every sense of the word, older than Maybella and indomitably cantankerous.

The place had two male roustabouts

who took care of drunks and other fractious customers, though there weren't too many of either: Maybella kept a good place of its kind.

Ginger Lil 'looked after' the girls. The two male plug-uglies (and the girls were far from ugly) were as much in terror of Lil as the girls were. She treated them all fairly though, Maybella made sure of that.

Lil had been looking after young Stefan in Maybella's absence: she was as fond of the boy as Maybella was and, to prove this, Stefan had brightened considerably, though he would not be able to ride. As had been already suggested by Torlando, a buckboard was the thing, and this was soon taken care of after Maybella was ensconced with Ginger Lil for a while in the back office.

Had any of the girls heard what passed between Maybella and her bosom friend in that private place they would have been mightily surprised.

The two madams would have been

shocked had they known that there was one of the girls — if only a small one — who heard part of their conversation and then slunk away. A filly who had recently received a tongue-lashing and a threat of expulsion from Lil for stealing from her colleagues.

Soon Maybella, Torlando and Stefan were ready to go; and Ginger Lil was left in the office alone, slumped over the ornate mahogany desk, her great body heaving as she wept bitter, lonely tears.

A surprising thing maybe, as Ginger Lil now owned, lock, stock and barrel — and the girls and roustabouts — the establishment that had always been known as Maybella's Place — and still would be, if in name only.

Maybella had been mighty prosperous but had never been as rich as she now was, though even Lil did not know how rich. Maybella was cutting all ties behind her and starting a new life with an old paramour, Pete Torlando, and with her surrogate son, Stefan. The local doc, a drunken but erudite man, had predicted that Stefan would get well but would be crippled, maybe severely, maybe not.

His welfare was in the hands of the fates — and Maybella and Torlando as, the sun on their backs, they moved further into Mexico, with the rain slowly easing.

★   ★   ★

The law bunch was still quite a way from its destination when the dun mare called Dusey began to act up, taking her rider, Perce, and the rest of the company, completely by surprise.

She rose on her hind legs and began to do a little dance, almost pitching the astonished Perce backwards out of the saddle. He held on, squawling, 'Hell, she's going loco!' She pirouetted and he lost the reins, found himself with his arms round the beast's neck, clinging, swearing.

Some of the boys laughed. It was the first time during a long, grim trail-ride that there had been any merriment, even a hint of it. But they couldn't help it. The sight of ol' Perce clinging to his horse like a veritable tenderfoot was too much for them.

Dusey did a sort of buck and wing, but as graceful as a ballet dancer, a personage that none of the boys had ever got to see; such culture was unknown in their slice of the wide South-west. One man screamed with a sort of hysteria, the tears running down his face — and Perce, finally unseated, left the saddle and ended up on his butt on the hard earth.

Another man, half-choking with merriment, managed to grab Dusey's reins and hold on. She settled down on all fours, glancing around her with big eyes kind of merry as if she looked for approbation, even applause.

Perce clambered to his feet, dusting himself down, going carefully at the rear end which felt like it was bruised. He raised his foot as if he would kick the horse; but then he lowered it again, stood watching her for a mite, scratching his head before turning, bending, picking up his hat and dusting that off.

'That goddam sodbuster,' said Ep Lamister. 'Where in hell would he get a hoss like that?'

'That man had a limp,' said Tubs Smildey. 'Did you notice that, Ep?'

The sheriff looked at him, dull-eyed. 'Cain't say that I did.'

'Maybe he was a performer once,' said Tubs. 'A circus or rodeo rider. A clown. Maybe he got crocked an' that's why he became a sodbuster.'

Ep had nothing to say to that. Perce was getting back in the saddle, and Dusey, her showing-off at an end it seemed, was as docile as an old-timer chawing baccy on his porch in the sun. And there *was* sun now and the rain was but a drizzle.

'You be good now, honey,' said Perce, gripping his reins tightly. He wasn't the sort to bear malice over such a thing as a fractious cayuse, and this one it seemed was a cayuse in a million.

The horse turned her head and looked up at him. 'I'll swear she winked at me, damn her hide,' Perce said. But she was looking straight ahead again and she moved as the others moved, as the sheriff said, 'C'mon, we're wasting time.' No merriment in Ep Lamister at all.

His friend Tubs had noted that Ep had pinned his lawman's star up on his breast, though the man was way out of his jurisdiction now and that law-badge had no clout in this territory at all.

Still, Ep was proud of being a star-packer, and one of the best of his kind. Tubs knew how his old friend felt. He raked out his own star and pinned it on.

When they reached Rancho Juanita the rain had stopped but the narrow streets — there were only two of them — ran with treacly black mud that made riding difficult. They were glad to light down at the sorry-looking livery stable. This outlaw town wasn't hot on amenities.

They split up. They made for

Maybella's Place, some at the front, some at the back. It wasn't too early for business. That might be just starting, after the girls, sleeping the morning out and some of the afternoon, rose and donned their glad rags. But these boys weren't looking for glad rags or the fillies who sported them.

Ep Lamister, with friend Tubs at his heels, marched right through the front door. Those two men, the big still-young sheriff and his slightly older deputy, knew that madam of old, and the madam's *segundo*, Ginger Lil, who met them in the surprisingly ornate lobby.

They knew that lobby all right, and Lil greeted them pleasantly, almost like old friends, her fat shaking, a wide smile fixed on her broad face with the green eyes. But those eyes were not twinkling now and their owner looked in a sorrowful mood, even as if she'd been recently weeping.

Ep, who lately had been acting like a cat with a scalded tail, took this up right off, demanded, 'What's up, Lil, huh?'

The answer came out as if forced from the big woman with the flaming red hair.

'Maybella's gone.'

'Where's she gone?'

'I don't know.'

They didn't believe her but, right now, there didn't seem to be anything they could do about that. Two of the boys came in from the back, with drawn guns, ushering the two roustabouts who had been relieved of their weapons: guns, knives, blackjacks. 'They got in our way,' one of the boys said.

Girls peeped. Until Lil growled at them. There were disappearances, stifled giggles.

'Let 'em go,' said Lil, meaning the two plug-uglies. 'They won't do anything.'

'We'll leave their gear with you when we leave,' Ep said. 'What else can you tell us?'

The two roustabouts had been let loose, weaponless. Their new boss had spoken; they weren't going to argue with her, or any of the determined-looking characters who seemed to have temporarily taken over the bordello.

'I can't tell you anything more,' said Ginger Lil. ''Cept I don't figure Maybella is coming back.'

Joey Danco hadn't been in evidence, only the two roustabouts. Ep asked about Joey, figuring he'd gone with Maybella, was surprised to learn that Joey was dead, killed by Pete Torlando, his old rival. And Torlando had gone with Maybella and they'd toted young Stefan along with them. And the boodle too, of course: Ep had to figure that.

Maybe Lil was telling the truth after all. It was highly probable that Maybella and the other two wouldn't be seen in Rancho Juanita again.

'Didn't she tell you anything at all?'

'Nope.' Lil shook her big, flaming head, vehemently.

They had to leave it at that. Sort of an anticlimax. They had half expected to meet with some shooting in this outlaw town. They had run into nothing except a sort of damp squib.

'You're running this place now then, Lil?'

'I am. It's all mine.'

That figured!

She went on. 'If you gents an' your friends want to avail yourselves, we'll . . . '

'We'll pass,' put in Ep. He and Tubs went through to the back to round up the boys.

Lil was chivvying curious girls, telling them to get ready for business, quit lolly-gagging.

One little thing with wild yellow hair went 'P-sss' to Ep while there was no other filly around. Ep looked surprised.

'Dru?'

'I know where they've gone, Sheriff. Maybella and Torlando. I heard Maybella telling Lil. They've gone to Priest's House.'

She disappeared. 'Who's the midget?' Tubs asked.

'I'll tell you later.'

'What's Priest's House? Hell, I know this town of old but I ain't never heard of somep'n called Priest's House.'

'It's way on,' said Ep. 'C'mon, let's move. I'll tell you while we ride.'

20

Ep seemed to have brightened somewhat but Tubs still didn't like the look of his friend's eyes. Still, the big, dark, tough lawman had always had heavylidded orbs, and, also, was wont to play his cards close to his chest. He'll be all right, Tubs told himself, wondering whether Ep still had a headache and that was all.

Ep began to talk, in spurts.

'It's all part of the same story I guess, you can look at it that way. There was a priest who lived in a house. Father Esteban. His church was adjacent, just a little place of clapboard an' adobe. The nearest settlement a mile on. Folks there were Esteban's parishioners, loved the old man. One night the church caught fire. Nobody knew how. Maybe a drunken *vaquero*, smoking a weed, letting the hot stub lie. Esteban ran out with water, tried to put the blaze out. The place fell in on him, killing him. The house which had always been called Priest's House by travellers, fell into disuse.

'There was an owlhooter called Obadiah Preece lit down there, price on his head in the States, had to stay in Mexico, decided to be a trader. Called the place Priest's House again, even called himself 'Priest', that being so near his own name. A comical killer, Priest. But you had to give him credit for one thing, a good business sense, and a hell of an ability to cut all kinds o' corners.

'He built a trading station, and a big house for himself. The old priest's house is still standing, though. The Mexican folk use it like a shrine, all good for business as far as Obe Priest is concerned. The rest is like a damn' fortress and Priest has a lot of gunnies under his banner, Mexicans, a few Anglos . . . '

'And that's where we're going,' said Tubs.

'It surely is, *amigo.*'

'So how about the midget filly with the yeller hair?'

'She's part o' the story too. Priest was married to an Anglo widder-woman for a while, her man a hiding-out gunfighter from Texas getting himself stabbed to death in a brawl in a cantina. The little yeller-haired girl was the woman's daughter. The woman died suddenly and Priest didn't want the kid any more. He treated her barbarously.

'She ran away, that's when I met her, in Rancho Juanita. Young Drusilla. Everbody called her 'Dru' o' course. She was fourteen then . . . '

'She don't look any more than fourteen now.'

'She's older than she appears to be. She was a skivvy for a cantina owner and his missus. Nothing much. A poor thing. But I guess they treated her a mite better than Priest had.' Ep blew out a gust of breath. 'I didn't figure she'd finish up in Maybella's Place, though it was inevitable I guess; warmth, companionship, whatever.'

★ ★ ★

Maybella and Torlando split up. The woman took the front, the man the back. They knew that Priest always had two men on watch, front and rear.

His main house would rival anything that any high-falutin' Spanish don had for himself and his family, though now Priest didn't have any family. But he had his two Anglo friends, his body-guard.

The front-man sat in a cane armchair on the spacious veranda. He rose when he saw Maybella approaching. He knew Maybella, had often journeyed to Rancho Juanita on his off-times and taken advantage of one or the other of her girls' particular brand of hospitality. He was a killer. But he was young and impressionable and, when the hand-some madam told him she had come to pay a friendly visit on her old friend,

Priest, he let her through.

The man at the back was older than his partner, but he knew Torlando of old, had once ridden with him for a while.

Torlando got near to him and pistol-whipped him extremely hard, then dragged him to a nearby outhouse and left him there.

Maybella was already shaking hands with long, lank Priest when Torlando appeared in the opulent sitting room. Priest turned, suspicious of the way Torlando had come in the back way and the feller out there hadn't announced him.

Priest wasn't wearing his gun but had one in his desk and he moved round there. Torlando wasn't fooled. He hadn't come in with his gun out, but his draw was a thing of wonder. Priest didn't have a chance. Torlando shot him in the middle of the forehead, sending him to disappearance behind his desk.

Maybella emitted a very unladylike exclamation, added, 'I didn't aim for you to kill him.'

'You cain't trust a snake like that,' Torlando said.

There was a clatter of boot-heels and the young front-man came through, a gun in his hand. But Torlando still had his weapon lifted. He pointed it at the new arrival like a steel finger and thumbed the hammer, twice, rapidly, not taking any chances.

The young man was stopped in his tracks as if he'd hit an invisible wall. He bounced, then he finished up in a strange curled position on the lush carpet. There was no more life in him any more.

Maybella and Torlando went out on to the veranda. Folks were coming across the beaten courtyard. Most of them were Mexican. Torlando held one hand high and these folk drew slowly to a halt.

Torlando shouted, 'There has been bad trouble here, some kind of a fight. Señor Priest and his two gunfighters are dead. Señora Maybella and myself will be in charge here, that was what would have been arranged with Señor Priest.'

The tall man paused, his head turned towards the left where on the edge of the gathered people, quite close, a white-haired old Mexican stood.

'Papa Juan, you know me.'

'I know you, Señor Torlando.'

'You know there will be more *dinero* for all. From me. And you know my good lady *amigo*, Maybella, who is also very straight.'

'I know, Señor Torlando. Señora Maybella.' The old man gave the handsome woman a small courtly bow.

'True, my friend Papa Juan,' Maybella said — and the day was won.

They had left young Stefan a few miles back at a smallholding owned by a one-legged *mestizo* who had ridden with Torlando a few times before he got wounded in an ambush with the Texas Rangers and only made the border in time. Stefan would be all right. The *mestizo*, known as Pemmican, had said that he would teach the wounded youngster to walk again, as he did himself although he only had one pin left to him to walk upon.

He was doing just this when the bunch of riders pulled in. Stefan wasn't doing too badly either but he eyed the newcomers with wide-eyed alarm, recognizing most of all Sheriff Lamister and his deputy, the one called Tubs. He liked them both but feared them also. They were, it might be said, the last people he wanted to see right then.

Each man wore a lawman's star pinned to his breast. The followers, some of whom Stefan began to recognize, were a stern, determined-looking bunch.

'Hallo, boy,' said Ep Lamister.

★ ★ ★

They had to have funerals, that was expected, they had to go along with that.

Nobody asked questions, not even other non-Mexicans, and there were a few of those. Including four Anglos and a couple of tame Yaqui Indians. Pete Torlando was well known and he had a lot of persuasive habits, some of which might turn lethal if he became too upset.

His lady *amigo*, Maybella, also well known, was quiet and handsome and suitably sad. She didn't wail like the other women, the camp followers, the few wives and mistresses.

Two graves. One for the two Anglo boys. And one alone for Señor Priest, once an *jefé*, now a shell. Papa Juan said a few words: that was fitting; Juan had known the original priest, Father Esteban. The weeping stopped. The clods fell. The folks dispersed. Not too long before a new morning, a new start; who could complain about that?

The darkness fell. There were camp-fires, an after-burying get-together.

Folks celebrating that they were still alive. Others had gone, never to return. Gone. *Gone*.

Plenty of pulque, mescal, tequila. All

sorts of concoctions of food and drink. Dancing. Singing. Twanging guitars. One of the Anglo boys had a squeeze-box and was pretty good at it.

At first Pete Torlando wasn't in evidence. Now the new *jefé*, supposedly he wasn't too keen on mixing too much with the menials. But Madam Maybella wasn't so particular. Men doffed their hats to her. Women looked upon her with favour: she was the best of their kind, the boss-lady.

She seemed to be spending a lot of time talking to Papa Juan, and both of them were sober. Torlando did put in a brief appearance. He had a few words with Maybella and Juan but didn't stay long. He didn't even take a convivial drink, not as anybody noticed. But maybe he had a bottle of prime bourbon back in his big house, and cigars and sweetmeats. The late — but now not so lamented — Obadiah Priest had indulged himself well.

Papa Juan was an old friend of Maybella's from way back in her own young days in the river and border regions. It could be said that Juan was an old friend of Torlando's also, but in a different way. Papa Juan, if he *could* be afraid of anything, could be afraid of Torlando, the great *bandido*. But Papa Juan had also been famous for his fearlessness, had in the old days led many raids for Priest.

Maybe the polyglot folk celebrating now were too drunk — or too stupid — to think on such matters now. But Pete Torlando certainly was not. Pete was a fiddlefoot, had never been used to staying in one place for very long.

He had enjoyed what he did. The raids, the chase, the trail, the danger: all this was in his blood. The stagecoach job had brought the richest haul he had ever known, at the cost of the folks who'd ridden with him. Like many of his kind he had dreamed of such a haul, had schemed for it. He'd come out on top. But now was the big let-down. Where did he go from here? Was this it? A ranch, a settlement, a quiet life? The gold converted to cash with folks he knew up-country where the North American law couldn't touch them or him. Then a quiet life . . . ?

No! He wanted to enjoy himself, gamble as he'd always gambled, have plenty of women, have folks looking up to him as he travelled, the notorious *pistolero*, Señor Torlando.

All that boodle . . .

He smiled at Maybella when she came in. She let him take her, there and then on the ornate *chaise-longue* which Priest had probably had brought here from New Orleans, some place like that.

She was naked when he dragged her hands behind her, preparatory it seemed for more love-making. But now he slipped a loop of rawhide over her wrists and pulled it tight.

Divining his intention, mighty savage at herself for giving way as she had, she kicked out at him. He laughed. Her bare feet could do him no harm. He pushed her to the carpet, her face in the thick pile.

He gagged her, trussed her legs, lifted her back on to the *chaise-longue*.

'I'm lighting out, honey,' he said. 'Hell, I can't stay here. This ain't my sort of thing. I should kill you. But we've had some good times. Besides, I ain't never killed a woman yet. I wouldn't want you to be the first.'

Her eyes blazed at him. She tried to talk but only mumbled. 'One o' the boys will find you,' he said.

He had got himself prepared. A horse. The boodle. Provisions. Everything he needed. The first leg of his journey wouldn't take him all that far anyway.

21

Papa Juan followed him a little way after seeing him leave, not galloping his horse till he hit the trail. The old Mexican saw which trail he took, figured what would be his first call along that trail then turned back to the camp. He was on the perimeter of the sleeping camp — there weren't even any guards — when he found himself surrounded by a bunch of horsemen.

They had come out of the night like ghosts, their horses' hooves deadened of sound by strips of rags tied around them.

Slowly. Only the guns gleaming, pointing at the astonished old man.

The big man at their head spoke softly, just said, 'Hallo, Papa Juan.'

There was a thin slice of moon, twinkling stars high in the sky above. Juan squinted, peered.

'Señor Lamister,' he said.

'The same, *amigo*. We don't want to awaken your *compadres*. We are looking for Priest and Maybella and Torlando.'

'Priest is dead. Torlando has lately ridden out, *Señor*. Maybella must still be in the house. We should look.' Juan was suddenly alarmed for the fate of the *señora* he liked so much.

★   ★   ★

Nobody challenged them as they moved to the house. They heard sounds. Maybella had chewed part of her gag away. She was spitting, her naked body uncoiling like springs as they unwrapped her. Torlando had done his job well, and cruelly.

'He's gone. He took everything.'

'We know,' said Sheriff Lamister, his star still gleaming on his broad chest.

'I theenk I know where he ees going, *Señor*,' said Papa Juan.

'Tell me.'

Juan told him. None of the other

209

boys had heard of the place before but Ep evidently had.

'Let's get going,' said star-packing Deputy Tubs Smildey.

'You're not goin', any of you,' said Ep. 'He's only one man now and I know that territory. He's mine.'

'But, Ep . . . '

'Enough! I know what I'm doin', what I want to do. You've backed me all along, all of you. I want you to get back home an' to your families. Those are my orders, and I'm still the boss-man. Am I not still the boss-man?'

Nobody argued about this, not even Tubs. Ep had always been the boss-man, and he certainly was the best gun-handler of them all. Tubs still felt that Ep wasn't quite himself, but he knew there was nothing he could do or say that would dissuade his friend from taking the path he'd chosen.

Maybella was dressed, standing silently, watching and listening. Tubs jerked a thumb. 'How about her?'

'Take her back. Pick up young Stefan

at Pemmican's place an' take 'em both back. Hell, I don't want 'em. Let 'em stay in Mexico back at Maybella's Place. Ginger Lil will be overjoyed to see 'em back there.'

'Thank you, Ep,' said Maybella. 'Back there it'll be the way as before, I promise.'

He didn't seem to hear her. 'Get going, all of you,' he said.

He sent Papa Juan back to his friends. He didn't leave the others, however, till after they left the camp and they all, Ep included, took the rags off their horses' hooves. The last thing Ep saw was the dun mare, Dusey, forked by Perce, doing her prancing bit before they disappeared in the night.

* * *

Ep did not drive his horse, just kept him going steadily, the way the gallant beast liked to go, covering the miles with a muscular steadiness. Ep still had a headache, didn't want to be jounced

211

too much in the saddle. He felt good enough, though, to face whatever would lie ahead of him.

He had an unswerving desire to finish what he'd started, even if it meant the finish of him also.

The night was not as sultry as it had been in very recent times. There was the slice of moon and the tiny stars high above it. Vision wasn't bad. The trail led horse and rider through flatlands with rock outcrops here and there at the sides, outcrops of mesquite and chaparral and stands of cottonwoods and other trees and vegetation. There were cacti but they were of a more shrivelled kind than those Ep had left behind in Texas.

Such a short time ago. But so much had happened. The end of this trail should be the end of it all. The end of something in which he now didn't want anybody else involved. He didn't chide himself for his selfishness, only felt good with himself because so far he had carried on as he'd planned to do after setting Maybella free in Priest's House; had set them all free.

But he had lost Denny, who had been like a son to him and for that he must make amends, exact revenge, payment from whom payment was due. And payment too for volunteer deputy, neighbour Caleb, an old friend, dead at the back door of the jail . . .

He figured he knew where Pete Torlando was heading. He figured that, strangely enough he, Ep, might have an advantage at that place. In his roaring youth he had spent wild times in this part of Mexico and, as far as he'd heard, times here hadn't changed much since the old days. This was not range or nesters' land, this was outlaw territory and, despite the star he still wore on his breast, he was an outlaw now. If things had not changed too much . . .

The trail was becoming all the more familiar. It was as if he was riding into the past.

A young man little more than a kid.

Crossing over the big river and, for the first time, delving into Mexico. Getting into a fight in a trailside cantina. (That place must be gone now, he thought.) Splitting a man's head, though learning later that the feller, a hotheaded Mexican boy, had survived. But his attacker young Ep, still running with the *rurales* on his heels. Seeing the big rocks. Hiding in them and being picked up by the outlaw bunch, who hated the *rurales* far more than this Anglo boy ever could.

The *bandido* leader, still a young man — a man called Bambito — taking Ep under his wing for a while, hiding him until he wanted to return to his home, to Canyon Pass. They had not met since, but Ep, becoming a lawman, had from time to time heard from other border law about Bambito and his mountainous hideout . . .

Dawn was putting a pale pink wash across the sky when he saw the so-familiar peaks again silhouetted against a backdrop, as if painted there by some great artist. Waiting, Brooding . . .

Back in the long time ago the luck had been with him. Would it be with him now?

He took off his star and dropped it into the pocket of his scuffed leather vest. He slowed his horse. The sky was becoming redder over the peaks. The dawn was opening to the morning.

The voice came from the peaks, but he could not see anybody.

'Stay where you are or I will shoot you down.'

He halted the horse. He shouted, 'I am an old friend of Bambito. Is he still there?'

'He is here.'

The voice sounded Anglo, but sort of stilted.

'Is Pete Torlando there?'

The question was not answered right off. Suddenly there were two voices and he could not hear what they said.

Then the stilted voice shouted, 'Pete

Torlando came last night. Who are you?'

It was a question that the man on the horse had been waiting to answer.

'My name is Ep Lamister. Tell Bambito I am here. Tell Torlando I am here. Tell him I will wait out here and he must come out alone, as I am alone, and bring his goods and his weapons and I will meet him face to face.'

His words died away in the still morning, and up in the rocks too, there was silence.

Ep waited. There were two men at least. Maybe one of them had gone with the message given to them.

Would Bambito remember and, if so, what would he do about the strange request? He was a thief and a killer but, like many of his kind, a man of strange loyalties, strange impulses and, at times, even a straight man.

Did he already know about Torlando's goods? Had he, in one way or the other, taken them?

Whether or not, would Torlando

want to prove himself? Would Bambito, intrigued, want him to do that, force him even, for the sake of an old friend? Would Torlando make the grandstand play anyway?

He thought about Bambito. Bambito, who could change gold into cash, who could change anything into *anything*. Who had had a great hacienda but, half Apache that he was, had returned to the hills that he loved, and the caves and the cabins. With his woman and himself having the biggest cabin of all from which they travelled incognito from time to time: New Orleans, Kansas City, Chicago, New York. Bambito had been reported captured; dead; Ep hadn't believed; was so glad now . . .

★ ★ ★

He waited longer than he had expected to, as the sun came up and he began to feel its heat. His patience had a sort of fatalistic quality about it.

But at last the man he was waiting for rode his horse down the rocks and there were two other men seen above now, with rifles, but these weapons were sloped, catching glints from the sun.

Pete Torlando reined in his mount on the flat ground and climbed down from the saddle, slowly, deliberately, as if he thought he still had plenty of time. Ep, seated comfortably till then, dismounted. His saddle was not so accoutred as the other man's was: Torlando had obviously brought his precious goods down with him. Like bait, Ep thought. *Like bait*.

Torlando was grand-standing now, hand-gun holstered low. Playing this out to the end.

He did not, however, stride forward as Ep would have expected him to do: as anybody would. He came away sideways from the horse. Maybe he was aiming to keep the sun out of his eyes. But it was more in Ep's eyes. He outfoxed me on that, Ep thought: he waited for the sun! But what could Ep have done?

Up on the peaks two men watched. Torlando halted as if in hesitation. He still looked forward at the waiting man but his lips did not move.

He turned and went back to the horse.

Ep saw the bursting flash of the sun on the metal of the long gun as Torlando took it from its saddle scabbard.

Damn his hide, he was going to use the rifle!

He was raising it.

Ep went into a crouch, lowering his long, heavy body, dipping his hand, reaching his pistol, his fingers gripping the warm, serrated butt. Hell, his rifle was back on his horse! Too late now! He stumbled — and the hot sun beat on his head. He heard the lead buzzing, the whiplash crack of the rifle; then he was on his belly, gun held out in front of him, pointing at the figure seeming so far in front of him, just a black shape.

The rest was instinctive: thumbing the hammer, twice, then rolling, punishing his damaged head. And then all he could see was the sun and he felt that his senses were leaving him.

He was still, but remaining on his belly, his senses returning. He felt kind of foolish. But — by Gar! — he was still alive. He saw the horse ahead, plainer than anything else he had seen. The four-legged shape shifting uncertainly, moving further away from the still form on the ground.

But then there was another figure, a human, upright, moving.

Ep raised the gun again.

'Hold it, *amigo*,' a voice called.

Ep hauled himself into a sitting position, his gun relaxed in his hand, the sun beating on his head. He couldn't see his hat anywhere. He squinted his eyes. His head drummed gently. Boot-heels shook the earth, stopped. A dark, grinning, bearded face looked down at him.

'It's only your ol' uncle,' the face said.

'I know,' said Ep. 'How are you, Bambito?'

'I ain't worried about me. You're *the man*. You got him. Twice in the chest. He's dead meat, an' I ain't worryin' about you any more. That was prime shooting.'

'Lucky shootin'.' Ep climbed shakily to his feet. 'An' me down on my gut like an old cur-dog.'

'Nah, this ol' cur-dog told you right.' Bambito poked a brown finger at his own wide chest.

Ep spotted his hat, bent, his head thudding, picked the wide-brimmed felt up and put it on his head. His horse stood waiting not far behind him. Ahead, Torlando's mount was patient also. The two men walked towards the horse and its dead master.

Bambito said, 'He didn't play it straight. You expected a straight stand-up two-pistol fight, didn't you?'

'Sure.'

'He used the rifle. Had he got you, though, my boys would've got him from up there.' Bambito jerked a big brown thumb up at the peaks. 'He wouldn't have got away with anything.'

Nothing, Ep thought. His life — nor the goods either! He looked at Bambito. Yeh, once this man had been like an uncle to him. His beard was thicker than Ep remembered it, and streaked with grey. Otherwise the old robber didn't look much different from when Ep had last seen him.

They were side by side over the body. Torlando was staring up into the sunny morning sky. Ep passed on to the horse, the sacks tied to the saddle.

'Them your goods?' Bambito asked.

'Yes.' Ep stretched a point. 'Torlando stole them. I have to take them back.'

'Rest, *amigo*.'

'I haven't time, old friend. But I will come and see you again. Now I must go. There are folks waiting.'

'I'll ride away with you, *amigo*.'

Bambito put two fingers to his mouth and emitted a shrill whistle. A saddled pinto with a black blaze across a white face cantered down from the rocks. There was no sign now of Bambito's two look-out marksmen.

The two men mounted up. Ep led the riderless horse.

The two men rode companionably side by side and did not talk. Neither of them had ever been loquacious types. They had heard about each other over the years. They had ridden side by side before like this. But that had been a long time ago . . .

They reined in where the trail forked.

Bambito reached out from his saddle to the riderless horse and slapped a large brown hand on the golden bulk there. He threw back his head and laughed. Then he said, thickly, 'I guess I must be getting back.'

Still grinning, he stared at Ep with dark eyes and shook his head slowly from side to side.

'Lucky cuss. Plumb lucky.'

'Now you told it true, old friend,' Ep said.

They both looked back as they went their separate ways. They saluted each other. Bambito still seemed to be grinning widely. But maybe that was just a trick of the sun . . .

Ep Lamister lost sight of his old friend.

As Ep, with his companions, the two horses, rode on the first leg of the trails that would take him home, he might have been heard to whisper, 'Yeh, *plumb lucky*!'

THE END

We do hope that you have enjoyed reading this large print book.

Did you know that all of our titles are available for purchase?

We publish a wide range of high quality large print books including:
Romances, Mysteries, Classics
General Fiction
Non Fiction and Westerns

Special interest titles available in large print are:
The Little Oxford Dictionary
Music Book, Song Book
Hymn Book, Service Book

Also available from us courtesy of Oxford University Press:
Young Readers' Dictionary
(large print edition)
Young Readers' Thesaurus
(large print edition)

For further information or a free brochure, please contact us at:
Ulverscroft Large Print Books Ltd.,
The Green, Bradgate Road, Anstey,
Leicester, LE7 7FU, England.
Tel: (00 44) **0116 236 4325**
Fax: (00 44) **0116 234 0205**

A TOWN CALLED TROUBLESOME

John Dyson

Matt Matthews had carved his ranch out of the wild Wyoming frontier. But he had his troubles. The big blow of '86 was catastrophic, with dead beeves littering the plains, and the oncoming winter presaged worse. On top of this, a gang of desperadoes had moved into the Snake River valley, killing, raping and rustling. All Matt can do is to take on the killers single-handed. But will he escape the hail of lead?